Behind the Magic 8 Ball

By

Amy Laprade

Behind the Magic 8 Ball

—Amy Laprade

Jumpy Jesse and Flighty Faith—two self-proclaimed wildlife activists—conspire to stop a fast food juggernaut from building on Jesse's childhood stomping ground: a cherished whiffle ball field and habitat to the Zebra-tailed lizard.

There's just one problem, Jesse's fear of 'just about everything' limits him to living vicariously through the heroic deeds of his favorite fictional character, George Hayduke—activist-turned-outlaw—of the novel, The Monkey Wrench Gang.

Faith's advocacy seldom extends beyond posting pictures of rehabilitated anteaters to her Facebook wall for the Wounded Anteater Reservation Project. She squanders her days watching reality TV in her pajamas instead of following through on life goals.

It seems that the Zebra-tailed lizard is doomed, until Jesse and Faith team up with Tanya, a firebug without a cause, but with a strategy to rescue the lizards from the ravages of Big Bang Burrito.

What strategy might that be? Will Jesse conquer his fears? Conquer himself? Will Faith come through for her cohorts? Is Tanya a hero or public enemy? Stay tuned to find out.

Acknowledgements:

First, I would like to thank Hazel Dawkins for having been such a supportive peer over the years, Richard Wayne Horton for his generosity toward peers within our Western Massachusetts writing community, Kathy Dunn of Main Street Writers for her nurturing spirit and for allowing me to speak my truth. Her workshop is one of a kind!

I wish to also thank the following who have given me pointers on how to make this book's opening scene shine off the pages: Kathy Dunn, Donald Fisher, Geoffrey Blüh, Albie Park, Stuart Mieher, Todd Walker, Roxanne Bogart, Kevin Cook, David Hollander, Olivia Warden, and the students of Justin Taylor's fiction workshop.

Also, a big thank you to Mary LaChapelle for not only believing in this project but for offering me such keen insight and wisdom as I worked to develop the characters and to give shape to the story.

Thank you Trish LaFreniere, Dolly Arsenault, William Drake, Nik Heikkila, Peter Williams, David Hunter, Joseph Kwiecinski. You have all been generous and instrumental with your feedback on previous drafts.

Thank you Ellen Eller for your sharp editorial skills and proof reading.

Thank you to the students of Grad Lab Theater Productions of Sarah Lawrence College. Because of you, I was able to witness scenes from Behind the Magic 8 Ball come alive as a stage performance—and to Michael Pollitt for giving me the chance to perform the novel's character sketches on WMCB-LP radio.

I would like to especially thank the following people:

Paul Richmond for being a key presence in the Franklin County arts community and for all the time and support he's offered to burgeoning writers.

Don Fisher whose seen me and been there for me over the years as I've taken this creative journey. You're the best!

Geoffrey Blüh for supporting me through it all and in every way. I love you!

This book is dedicated to Kathy Dunn, for her generosity and un-wavering support, and to Main Street Writers' Thursday night gang for their high energy, enthusiasm and good vibes. This book is also dedicated to Donald Fisher for being an important part of my cre-ative journey and to Geoffrey Blüh for being my rock.

Published by Human Error Publishing
www.humanerrorpublishing.com
paul@humanerrorpublishing.com

ISBN: 978-09973472-4-1

Cover Photography
Geoffrey Blüh

Cover Design
by
Amy Laprade and Paul Richmond

Illustrations by Amy Laprade

Author portrait by Geoffrey Blüh.

Table of Contents

Un-American

Jesse Timorlan had once fought to preserve the beauty of America's landscape by burning down highway billboards and blowing up dams—all from the safety of his couch and his imagination since, truthfully, he was too scared to even join a climate march. Just the thought of cops arriving in paddy wagons to spray the masses with a hot, peppery gas had made him so nervous, he felt like wetting his pants.

He chose, instead, to exude his rebellion by giving a presentation of his favorite novel: The Monkey Wrench Gang by Edward Abbey, which was set in the swinging 1970s and was centered on Jesse's idol, George Hayduke: environmental activist-turned-outlaw.

While Jesse stood stammering at the front of the classroom, Tanya, a chunky girl who had never once spoke during class, gazed out the window. Bruce, who always had a point to make and often spoke out of turn, sat with his feet on his desk. He sneered at Jesse and snorted, "You suck," between bites of food. His hoody, emblazoned with a bald eagle and the words "Home of the Brave," was pulled over his head in order to hide his activities. He was chowing down on the Bean-Me-Up-Scotty, a popular item from Big Bang Burrito's dollar menu. He was a loud eater and he made huge sucking sounds as he slurped his Comet Cola-Big-Slurp.

"George Hayduke, the n...novel's main p...protagonist, is a h...hero," Jesse continued. "Because he attempts to rescue the beauty of the desert from the ravages of commercialism by committing acts, which today might be d...deemed acts of terrorism, but which I think are n...necessary, in order for life to c...continue."

"C...c...continue," mocked Bruce. He glared at Jesse. He liked to glare at people, especially Jesse who preached the tenets of a tofu diet and wore T-shirts emblazoned with "Eat More Kale"—and who also liked to quote Edward Abbey. Jesse's taste in food and authors, Bruce felt, threatened the American way. Bruce's father, a retired logging tycoon, had ingrained in Bruce that it was his God-given, inalienable right to grab and grab and grab.

Jesse left class five minutes early in order to avoid a possible confrontation with Bruce. He was reminded, as he bolted for the bus shelter, how not green the campus had become. A patchwork of freshly paved parking lots was stitched together by concrete curbs and surveillance cameras. Yucca Community Way, which led to the lots, was also freshly paved and had signs posted every two feet, bleating SMILE, YOU'RE ON CAMERA! to all who entered.

To make matters worse, a row of newly constructed tract homes dominated the edges of Yucca Community Way where patches of mesquite grass had once flourished. Once the grass vanished, so had the families of white-tailed deer. No longer would Jesse observe them foraging at dusk while he waited at the bus shelter for the 15 to arrive.

The hard, plastic seat inside the shelter felt cold against Jesse's boney butt. He gazed beyond the glass at what little view remained: slivers of pink sunset wedged between the peaked rooftops of the tract homes. The sight of it made his pulse race, so he closed his eyes and tried to focus on his breath, but the non-stop whine of internal combustible engines penetrated his ears.

The highway, which intercepted Yucca Community Way, had once been a lonely, languorous road that ran to the edge of the earth, with only the occasional motorist stopping in Yucca to gas up before heading to wherever it was he or she was headed.

Jesse watched the 18-wheelers scream past, some transporting old-growth logs, others transporting hazardous materials—these had silver, tubular bodies that brandished the flammable liquid symbol and were the kind that frightened Jesse. But they fascinated him, too, as they were the kind that exploded in action thriller movies that his older brother, Gerald, liked to watch.

The sound of boots on pavement caught Jesse's attention. Bruce's hulking shape was fast approaching. It was unusual to see Bruce at the bus shelter, since he was known for burning rubber out of the student lot while shouting, "Pansy!" at Jesse from the window of his Ford pickup.

As Bruce was about to say something, a bus rolled up to the curb. The doors hissed open. Jesse, fear numbing his brain, absently boarded and took the seat behind the driver. Bruce, to Jesse's dismay, plunked down in the seat behind him.

Great, he knows my route. He knows my routine. Does he know where I get off? Where I live?

Jesse realized that he had nothing to fear as far as that was concerned. The route number posted above the door said, 51 PETRIFIED FOREST VIA DOWNTOWN, instead of 15 PRICKLY PEAR GARDENS EXPRESS, which would have deposited him safely to his doorstep.

Gosh, where will this bus take me? Area 51? Will I be abducted by aliens? Jesse could barely feel Bruce's fetid breath on his neck as he bit his nails and crossed his legs. He had to pee.

Bruce pressed his knees into the back of Jesse's seat. Jesse ignored the pressure digging into his back. He was busy surveying the scenery that'd flashed by and trying to decipher where it was that they were headed. However, dusk had faded to black, and all that Jesse could see in that sea of neon pollution was a reflection of his own freckled face and his own dazed eyes, looking much like those of the deer that'd grazed in the mesquite grass.

He pressed his nose to the window. Route 51 looked almost exactly like Route 15. This side of Yucca, the East side, had everything his side, the West side of Yucca, had: Barnes & Noble, Target, Starbucks, Home Depot, Walmart and another Big Bang Burrito—a fast food eatery currently under construction, not far from his house.

He wondered if the 51 would make an alternate loop that would eventually bring him by Prickly Pear Gardens. But when the bus merged onto a six lane highway, parted by a concrete divider with three lanes of traffic barreling one way and three lanes of traffic barreling the other, his hopes were dashed.

The last stop brought Jesse and Bruce to the corner of Petrified Forrest Lane and Tumbleweed Terrace. They were the last passengers. The craggy-faced driver grew impatient as Jesse, close to tears, withered in his seat, arms shielding his head while Bruce yelled, "Terrorist!" in his face.

"I...uh...h...have...um...p...pepper spray and I'm n...not afraid to u...use it," Jesse sniveled.

"Alright, break it up you two!" the driver barked.

As Bruce disembarked, Jesse had an epiphany: keep a clean nose in the presence of Bruce—in other words, Jesse would need to keep his un-American ideas to himself.

The Biggest Loser...

...had always been Faith's favorite TV show. She'd seen every episode of every season and had become crestfallen to learn that the show had stopped airing. Undaunted, however, she'd begun streaming reruns of the show from her Hulu account, late into the afternoons while still in her pajamas—the same ones she'd been wearing for days.

Faith was streaming reruns again, and was sucked into an episode where Bea, her favorite contestant, confesses to having gorged herself on "Bean Me Up Scotties" for three consecutive nights before the weigh-in. A replay of the previous episode shows Bea bearing a hangdog expression as one of her teammates finds her in the kitchen, at 2 a.m., with salsa dribbling down her chin, looking not unlike Sylvester with Tweety caught in his mouth.

Bea went on to explain to her other teammates how the "Bean Me Up Scotties" gave her the trots, which impeded her ability to run the obstacle course that the coach had set up for the red and the blue team. Another replay boasted a closeup of Bea's face twisted in agony as sweat dripped from her nostrils. The camera panned out to show her wheezing and grunting as she struggled to run. That day, Faith had had an earworm of "Chariots of Fire," and it'd cycled through her head during the entire episode while she cheered Bea on, from the couch.

Faith became outraged and offended when she realized that the film crew hadn't bothered to edit out the fart noise. The baritone toot that'd slipped out of Bea's rear as she tried to clear a hurdle—and missed—was now immortalized before an audience of millions and had gone viral. Worse, Bea gained back the ten pounds she'd worked so hard to lose.

Faith hung her head in defeat, as she had the last time Bea waved a tearful farewell to her companions on the blue team, before waddling off stage and back into her old life in Kermit, Texas.

Faith lifted her head, finally, when her phone continued to vibrate. She dared herself to glance at the caller ID:

BIG BANG BURRITO

She rolled her eyes and mumbled, "Yeah?"

"..... ....?"

"Oops, forgot I was covering for Marcos."

"... ....!"

"Okay. Okay. Yup—"

"... ....?!"

"Hey, I said I was sorry...I realize this is the second time I've forgotten but I've got a lot on my plate...be there in an hour—"

".. .. ....?! .. .."

"It does take an hour `cause I gotta ride the bus...can't drive `cause I gotta a hole in my muffler. I've been pulled over twice. I'll get there when I get there."

She knocked a stack of overdue bills from the arm of the couch as she got up. She kicked at the pile of dirty laundry en route to the bathroom. She slipped into her sour work clothes from the day before, of which she'd thrown onto a stack of magazines: old issues of Bust and Spin, which cluttered the top of her hamper.

There was a column about The Killers in an issue of Spin. Faith had the hots for Brandon Flowers who she thought looked a lot like Todd, a guy she'd dated for two months and then stopped calling. She'd even ignored Todd's texts. She didn't know why she suddenly started avoiding him or why she didn't just say, "I'm not interested anymore."

Perhaps it was because forthrightness gave her acid reflux, or so she thought, biting into a stale, Boston Cream donut.

Aside from the fact that Todd looked like Brandon Flowers, Faith didn't know why she dated Todd in the first place. Maybe it was because she was in love with the idea of him rather than that she was in love with him. She liked the way that the girls at Southwest University had stared at her in envy whenever she and Todd would eat lunch together. It made her feel important.

That was all history. She'd dropped out of school. Economics hadn't been her thing, too much math. Before that, it'd been botany. That hadn't been her thing either, too many science classes. She'd considered majoring in social justice but knew that'd take years of school—it'd already taken her four years to earn her certificate in Environmental Sustainability. For now, she was working the 24-hour drive-up window at a Big Bang Burrito while taking pottery classes at Yucca Community College. Her pottery class was to happen tomorrow but she was tempted to blow it off, thinking that she might feel too zonked to finish the toilet brush holder she'd been making for her mother's 60th birthday—which had already gone by. Besides, her sister Eileen, who Mother had always favored, had already thrown a surprise party for Mother at Eileen's oversized mansion, one with an in-ground pool and hot tub.

Faith paused in the lemon yellow sunlight which warmed the linoleum floor of her tiny studio, hemming and hawing. Go? Don't go? The arms on the kitchen clock were ticking away. Big Bang Burrito was waiting. A normal person would have waited to see how she felt the following morning before deciding about pottery class, but Faith didn't operate that way.

It was silly reaching for the Magic 8 Ball, she knew, but it beckoned her from atop of the fridge. She'd been trying to wean herself off the thing, but without it her life the past few days had been a mess. Yesterday, she couldn't decide which to do first, go to the laundromat or go food shopping without first consulting the ball. She tried to make up her mind all on her own but had an anxiety attack before she could even get her shoes on.

At first, Faith had liked the Magic 8 Ball for nostalgic reasons. She'd rescued it from her mother's attic several months ago. It'd belonged to her sister Eileen when they were kids. Faith remembers how fascinated she'd felt by the way that Eileen would shake it while asking life's big questions: did Brad, the paper boy on their street, have a crush on her as she did him? Should she invite the weird chick with braces to her sleepover? Would she achieve straight As on her report card this quarter, as she had every other quarter?

Of course Eileen got straight As that quarter, and as Faith recalled, the ball had predicted that she would when its icosahedron die floated to the blue watery surface to say,

It is Certain.

And so, Eileen's report card was proudly displayed on Mom's refrigerator while Faith's was fed to Hamburglar, her pet guinea pig. Faith had felt certain that if she had just had a chance to ask the

19

ball a question, she could have dodged getting a D in math—but she wasn't allowed anywhere near Eileen's ball, in the same way she wasn't allowed anywhere near Eileen's diary.

Nevertheless, the ball sat on top of Faith's fridge, a glossy orb beaming down at her, the sunlight glinting off of its shiny blackness. She then made a compromise to herself that she'd at least wait until she boarded the 15 before consulting it. She pulled on her tennis shoes, slipped the ball into her Jansport bag and stepped out.

A Real Revolution

Jesse waited inside the shelter for the bus that would take him to Yucca Public Library. He was to borrow a field guide on desert animal dung, to see if he might identify the mysterious droppings that had turned up in his yard—although they were probably compliments of Yucca's vagrants, who tended to treat the Timorlan's yard like an outhouse. One time, one very drunk vagrant mistook his mother's birdbath for a public urinal.

While waiting for the bus, Jesse watched the construction happening across the street. His father and brother Gerald were among the workers adding the finishing touches to the new 24-hour Big Bang Burrito—plopped down on Jesse's childhood stomping ground: a field where he'd played whiffle ball as a kid. The field had once teemed with desert tortoises, jackrabbits and monarch butterflies. Each spring, after a dusting of rain, the field's fuchsia-tinted blossoms would spring from the rubbery, thorny tips of the prickly pear cacti that'd dotted the field.

Jesse reminisced about the sunny afternoons spent poised in that field, and the way that his freckled forehead would bake in the dry heat—how his eyes would squint as the whiffle ball came barreling down from the sky's blue depths. "Catch it, Jesse!" His teammates would yell.

But he would be too nervous to catch that ball. Always, it would bounce out of his grasp and then off the boulders, making a THWACK as it did so. The zebra-tailed lizards that'd been sunning themselves moments before, would dart from the boulders and into the shadows. Jesse had been glad to see them go.

However, he was not glad to see the field go, which had remained pristine and unspoiled until two months ago when a backhoe appeared. Jessie had arrived at the bus stop to discover that the field had been yanked inside out, and had morphed into a mountain of stones and iron-tinted sand. The sidewalk that'd bordered the field was slashed open like a municipal wound, exposing a network of sewer pipes and gas lines. Jesse had pictured the baby bunny rabbits peacefully slumbering in their dens, deep below the sidewalk, but then bolting and running for their dear little lives as the jackhammers fired their first holes into the concrete.

Next came the whine of the saws as the prefab walls went up. That day, Jesse had had to increase the volume on his iTunes so that he could hear the lyrics to John Denver's "Rocky Mountain High."

Today the workers were building a walkway to Big Bang Burrito's entrance. The cement truck made a BLEEP, BLEEP, BLEEP sound as it backed up, and then an earsplitting PFFT as the driver hit the breaks. The portly drum made its slow rotation while spitting a gray slurry onto the chute. Sunlight glinted off Dad and Gerald's orange hard hats as they smoothed out the fresh, wet concrete with their trowels. The other workers barked orders at each other, only Jesse couldn't hear what they were saying over the growl of the cement mixer. He imagined that some colorful swear words were tumbling from their lips.

A landscaper would later plant barrel cacti along Big Bang Burrito's walkway—all the other restaurants had them. The old-growth saguaro—home to a family of elf owls—was to be pulled from the ground in order to make room for the yellow neon sign, which vaguely resembled Saturn and bore Big Bang Burrito's insignia.

Jesse had no idea how the restaurant chain had managed that one, since the state of Arizona had strict regulations about cutting down saguaros. The cactus removal would happen just before the grand opening—he knew this because Dad and Gerald discussed work, incessantly, each night over dinner.

"Yucca doesn't need a fourth BBB," Jesse had insisted, while also recalling that he'd come down with the worst stomach cramps after having eaten the "Bean Me Up Scotty."

"New construction equals money. You can't eat whiffle ball fields, Jesse," Dad had countered, clutching a turkey drumstick in his grubby fingers. He took an enormous bite. Jesse understood then that this was his cue to drop the subject.

"Yeah, Nature Valley Boy," piped Gerald, mashed potatoes flying from his lips as he spoke. "Why don't you go to your room and eat a granola bar?"

While reflecting on the conversation, Jesse tried to picture elf owls building a nest out of the Big Bang Burrito sign. The thought of the doomed saguaro with its brood of displaced owls turned his stomach. The restaurant would be cutting the ribbon and having another grand opening celebration in only two days. Jesse could imagine the smell of helium inside the party balloons, the taste of confetti on his tongue, and the whisper of loneliness at his feet while Dad and Gerald had a celebration of their own—one he wouldn't be invited to—that entailed a surf and turf dinner at the newly constructed Outback Steakhouse, which had been built over a wetland Jesse used to birdwatch in—until he encountered a dia-mond-backed rattlesnake and wet his pants. A surf and turf dinner was a ritual of Dad and Gerald's upon completion of every job.

I don't need to be a part of either celebration—just a part of a revolution. One to rescue the planet.... But who would join his revolution?

"Dude, doesn't this make you sick?"

A female voice interrupted Jesse's thoughts. He looked up and saw Faith, a scatty, frizzy-haired girl he knew from pottery class, although not very well, since she seemed to be absent a lot. She jerked her thumb at the construction site before slouching into a seat in the bus shelter. "Doesn't it like make you wanna vomit?"

"Oh...uh...yeah, sure...it makes me wanna...piss...uh...I mean puke my...pants...I mean it m...makes me sick, too." Jesse felt his face flush. He had to pee. Funny, the need hadn't been there until Faith sat down. "Like...I hate Big Bang Burrito too—"

"They have the dough to build another dumpy 24-hour restaurant but won't pay me more than ten bucks an hour... then they have the gall to slash my hours so I can't get health insurance...then they expect me to be on call...." Faith trailed off as she considered her attitude toward the new restaurant.

Although if they transfer me to this new store I'd only have a five-minute walk to work instead of a 15-minute drive...although it'd be harder to play hookie because I'd likely be spotted by a co-worker....

"Someone ought to start a revolution...a real revolution... forget 'Fight for 15.' I say down with commercialism!" Faith pumped her fist. "Although a revolution seems like a lot of

24

work." Faith let her fist fall into her lap. "Maybe someone should just organize a walk out."

"Uh...would...you uh, wanna...like...j...join my um, radical movement...if I...were, uh, to start one?" Jesse began biting his nails.

Faith shot Jesse a puzzled look as she tried to understand how a quiet boy, who seldom made a peep during pottery class, had the gall to suggest such an idea.

"Uh...I realize h...how uh...bad that sounds...but...uh... it's not like we'd be...uh, killing people and stuff. We'd be...um...protesting the new BBB and we'd uh...march in the streets...and uh...hold picket signs that say, 'BBB's employees don't wash their hands—'"

"I wash my hands," Faith huffed, directing her gaze away from Jesse to the netted side-pocket of her Jansport bag, at her job resume rolled up and held together with a rubber band. She had planned to drop it off at the SPCA, before she realized that it had a coffee ring on it.

"Or," Jesse quickly added, positioning his eyes on his tennis shoes. "Like...we could, um...hold picket signs with illustrations of uh...black beans with eyes and ten sets of legs...you know? Like, to represent the idea that BBB uses genetically modified beans?"

Faith shifted her gaze to the cloudless sky, Jesse's proposal having sent her brain's cogs reeling back to a day, ten years ago, when she participated in the Fight for Family Farms March—until the blister on her pinky toe forced her back to the bus.

Thanks to the march, Jodd's Family Farm, nestled on two acres of land between Ayrhed International Airport and Yucca Shopping Center—once slated for development—was still in operation. Its Jersey cows had gone on to become the poster children of Cholla County's free range craze and were known to stop air-traffic whenever they foraged too close to the runway of Ayrhed International. Faith was proud to have donated 30 minutes of her life on behalf of this important historical moment.

"So...uh...like...uh...what do you...um...think?" Jesse squeezed his loins, wondering if Faith would be offended if he took a leak behind the bus shelter.

The Magic 8 Ball, tucked securely inside of Faith's bag, made splishy-splashy sounds as she pulled it into plain view, pressed her eyes shut and gave it a shake, murmuring, "Should I tag along with Jesse while he forms his radical movement? Is this where my life is meant to go?" She waited for the die to bequeath her an answer in the ball's watery window.

Concentrate and Ask Again.

Chewing her bottom lip and furrowing her brows, Faith shook the ball again while Jesse scratched his head appearing nonplussed. The die swiveled inside the ball's amniotic cell before delivering to Faith its second prophecy.

As I see it, Yes.

"Yeah, man, why not? Sounds like a super cool idea..." as long as I don't have to do much. "Got any ideas as to how you might ruin business for BBB?" Faith grinned. She and Jesse had barely noticed the chunky girl, who, dressed in paint-spattered overalls, leaned against the glass of the bus shelter, her teeth clamped around an deactivated vape pen.

"Uh..." Jesse cleared his throat. "We could, uh...like...glue the doors shut to every Big Bang Burrito in town—"

"Not to burst your bubbles or anything, but your lame-ass stunt isn't gonna touch a billion-dollar corporation," the chunky girl grunted, the vape pen quaking between her teeth.

Jesse wheeled around. It was Tanya from his English class, the girl who sat at a desk next to his and stared out the window during every lecture and never spoke, but who received an A on every project. Jesse copied her notes whenever he thought she wasn't looking.

Faith knew Tanya, but only vaguely. She was a fixture at Jittery Jo's—Yucca's only Mom and Pop cafe and Faith's favorite haunt. Tanya never talked to anyone, including Faith, but was often embroiled in a game of chess against Faith's friend, Josh.

Tanya would stare intently into the chess board, lips clamped around an unheated vape pen, her forehead furrowed in concentration as if by some mental will the chess pieces would come alive and start to move on their own. Her eyes would narrow on her choices as she gripped her bishop between sweaty fingers. Her final move of the game would occur swiftly and unexpectedly when she uttered, "Checkmate." She seldom lost a game.

Tanya knew Faith, but only vaguely. Faith was the only one from Jittery Joe's hipster crowd who didn't stare at the port wine stain on her chin as if it were a form of skin rot caused by a spider bite. Lots of people stared. Tanya felt sure of this, for she had received dirty looks on her way to the bus stop from mothers yapping on their cellphones as they pushed their babies in double strollers.

"It'll take more than some feather-brained idea to sink Big Bang Burrito. It's too big," Tanya grunted as she leaned against the bus shelter, vape pen dangling from the corner of her lips.

"Should we wait, then, for Big Bang Burrito to hit an iceberg and sink? That'd be a lot easier," Faith beamed. Jesse picked his nose. They looked at one another, nodding in agreement.

Tanya frowned."Or just destroy BBB yourselves."

Jesse flicked a booger from under his fingernail. He looked from Faith to Tanya. "Do you...uh...wanna join our...uh...radical group?"

"Let's discuss this in an intelligent manner and not in a public place." Tanya tucked her vape pen in her breast pocket.

"Does this mean you wanna join?" Jesse wiped his finger on his corduroys. He gazed anxiously at the vape pen wondering if it was any healthier than smoking. He wondered if the pen was activated. Vaping wasn't allowed in Yucca.

"Where are you two off to, anyway?" She asked.

"Uhh..." Jesse stammered. "Uh...I was gonna, uh—"

"I was on my way to work," said Faith, "but I don't think I'm gon-na—"

"Great," said Tanya. "My place. Right now."

Bury My Heart at Wounded Owl

With its fake grass and plastic daisies, there was nothing welcoming at all about the WELCOME mat on Tanya's stoop. Jesse noted this as he, Tanya and Faith entered the front hall, damp and smelling vaguely of mildew, tuna fish and mothballs. The house was hemmed in by a stand of tall Junipers, except for its north side, which contained a view of the highway. Thus, it felt chilly and damp inside.

The three entered the narrow kitchen where a fat, black cat, sat perched on the windowsill, and an old woman sat at the table, her head bowed over a crossword puzzle. The cat leapt to the floor, arched its back and hissed at Tanya as she lumbered toward the refrigerator.

"Fuck off, Freddy!" Tanya yelled in the cat's face.

Jesse and Faith remained in the doorway. They exchanged looks. Faith raised a brow, glanced at the old woman, who hadn't looked up. Freddy hissed again, his ears pressed to the sides of his head as he swatted Tanya's ankle.

"Pssst! Beat it!" Tanya hissed back at Freddy. She slammed her heel into the floor and the house shook. The cat ran. The woman still had not looked up.

Tanya strode toward the table. She poked the woman on the shoulder. The woman's head snapped up. The woman clapped her hands to her chest as if she was going into cardiac arrest. Tanya waved an exaggerated hello as a scowl spread across the woman's sunken lips. "Yew scare me, Tanna. I didn' even see yew coming!"

Judging from her odd speech patterns, and the fact that she'd seemed oblivious to her visitors, Jesse guessed that the woman was deaf. He waited for Tanya to make introductions. She did not. Instead, she opened the refrigerator and swigged from a two liter bottle of Dr. Pepper.

Jesse waited for her to offer him a drink. She did not, although she paused as she was about to close the refrigerator. "Oh...did you guys want some?"

"N...no...uh, thanks." Jesse never drank pop. Not that it mattered, since he was terrified of drinking from the same bottle. Faith shook her head. She loved pop, but she swore she saw Tanya backwash.

The woman struggled out of her chair. She tottered over to Faith and Jesse. "Ello, my name's Ginger, an' yer names are...?"

Jesse and Faith stepped around Tanya, now rummaging through the cabinets, in order to make introductions. Jesse noticed, as he took Ginger's hand, that it was frail as a bird's wing. The flesh of her palm was warm and spongy.

"Goooo to meet yew."

"Good. To. Meet. You. Too," Jesse said loudly, his lips dramatically forming the words, to ensure that Ginger would understand him.

Tanya grabbaed a bag of Cheetos from the cupboard. She jerked her chin toward a door off the kitchen. "Downstairs."

"Gotta go." Faith smiled vapidly at Ginger.

The mustiness was stronger in the basement. It nearly sent Jesse into a sneezing fit. Fluorescent bulbs, mounted along the ceiling, lit the way to a washer and dryer room, which opened onto a much larger room.

Inside the larger room, there was a glass display case along one wall, looking not unlike the jewelry cases Jesse had seen in department stores. Only, instead of jewelry, he was surprised to discover a knife collection inside, 25 total: a Swiss pocket knife, a butterfly knife, a hunting knife...his heart stopped when he saw the one with an ivory handle. It was a type of switchblade—likely to be illegal in all 50 states. He and Faith exchanged looks. Faith's smiling face went deadpan.

"Take a seat. Ya'll act like I'm psychopath." Tanya took a pull from her vape pen, tapped the play button on her tablet, and flopped down in the bean bag chair. "Do my knives freak you out?"

Silence. Nothing was heard but the keyboard intro of "Time to Pretend," by MGMT, plinking out of the tiny Bluetooth speakers.

"Let me guess, you never met a chick with a knife collection? No worries. I just think they're pretty."

Jesse sat on the edge of the futon. He crossed his legs. He had to pee.

Faith raised a brow. *It's not just the knife collection, it's that she's smoking indoors! In the town of Yucca, getting caught vaping indoors, even if it was inside one's own home, could land one in jail for 30 days, or a fine of up to 1,000 dollars.*

"It could be worse. I could have a pet tarantula or something." Tanya laughed, then fell silent. "So, let's see...how might we destroy the new BBB?" She said this in a way that sounded more like a question to herself. "Actually, let's talk about why it is you two want to destroy it."

"It sounds like fun." Faith shrugged. She dug her phone out of her Jansport bag.

"I agree, but why? Usually a person has a motive for doing what she does...she holds a very strong grudge..." Tanya exhaled smoke, a faraway look shadowing her features.

"They keep me at part time so I can't get health benefits...and the pay's lousy. Sure, I get perks but all the free "Bean Me Up Scotties" I can eat aren't paying my bills," Faith said, looking down at her phone.

Tanya crossed her legs. They were hairy. She caught Jesse wrinkling his nose at them. She saw him blush as he realized that he'd been caught. Tanya didn't care.

"I know why I hate BBB." She gazed dreamily at the network of pipes running in all directions before vanishing into the ceiling. The kitchen was directly above. She could hear the thunk of Ginger's cane and the swish-swash of her slipper-clad feet making contact with the floor. She could hear the pitter patter of Freddy running. The cat followed Ginger everywhere.

"Why...uh...do you...uh...hate it?" Jesse crossed his arms, partly because of the chilly damp—he was trying to stay warm—but partly because of nerves. The basement felt like a dungeon to him.

Tanya shook her head, her gaze never leaving the ceiling. "I asked you first—"

"What difference does it make!? I just hate it! I don't know!"

Faith looked up from her phone. She'd begun playing Candy Crush Saga with a Facebook friend. Wide-eyed, she glanced at Jesse as if startled from a deep sleep.

Tanya dragged her eyes off the ceiling. She looked directly at Jesse. Jesse, suddenly afraid of Tanya, and of his own outburst, started to cry.

"Tell me why it is you're crying," Tanya said, in a voice exuding as much emotion as Siri.

Jesse was thinking about the saguaro in front of the new Big Bang Burrito, soon to vanish along with its brood of owls. Its impending demise had triggered a memory of Jesse's camping trip at Owl Creek Canyon from when he was just ten-years-old.

Jesse and Gerald had gone about pitching their tents in the great outdoors while their father went into town to get more beer. Jesse chose to pitch his Sponge Bob pup tent next to the 20-foot-tall saguaro, at the edge of the campsite. He had been looking forward to gazing through the netted opening, at the majestic plant specimen which would be silhouetted against the planetarium sky come nightfall.

"Bet you're too chicken to shoot that owl," Gerald pointed a beefy finger at a pair of yellow eyes peering down at them from a hole in the saguaro.

"But...uh...like...uh...why would I...um...shoot it? It...uh... didn't do nothin' to me." Jesse regretted the prepubescent squeak in his voice. It was one feature among many that made him a target for Gerald's teasing.

"Take a shot or I'm gonna start calling you Jessica." Gerald handed him the rifle.

Being named Jesse after Jesse James—because Dad loved outlaws—had been fine with Jesse. There was just one problem. Outlaws weren't targets for playground bullies—and older brothers—and they didn't play jump rope at recess.

With a groan, Jesse took the rifle. He knew how to use it—he'd been dragged to the shooting range many times since the age of eight—he just didn't feel like shooting baby elf owls. He would rather observe them through binoculars. He would rather observe kangaroo rats or even a roadrunner—if he was lucky enough to catch a glimpse of one as it darted off into the sunset. He would rather identify desert animal dung with the help of his field guide. To begin with, he didn't like the sound of guns going off. At least the shooting range provided ear muffs.

Jesse hands shook when he pulled the trigger. He cringed as the sound of gun cracks ricochetted off the mountains. The bullet flew...somewhere...achieving nothing except to scare the owl into ducking deep into the hole, which is

32

what Jesse had hoped would happen.

"You're such a pansy. Gimme the gun," Gerald barked. They waited.

When the owl returned, Gerald took aim.

Jesse cowered behind his brother, hands clapped over his ears, eyes squeezed shut, silently rooting for the owl's escape while holding his bladder.

CRACK. The owl ducked back into the hole.

"Leave it, alone, Gerald!"

"Shut your cake hole, Jessica." Gerald sneered. He aimed... CRACK.

The owl ducked again and remained hidden somewhere in the depths of that ancient thorny edifice.

"Fuckin' rascal. You don't come out. I'll force ya out!" Gerald pulled a Rambo maneuver by firing non-stop, stitching a row of bullet holes along the lower half of the saguaro.

Jesse glanced anxiously down the dirt road, hoping to see plumes of dust over the horizon, which would signal their father's return in the rattly Ford pick up, but instead saw wispy clouds, lazily sailing the afternoon skies, indifferent to the plights of cacti and baby owls.

Jesse guessed that the other desert creatures were wisely huddled behind boulders—under lockdown from the sun's nuclear blaze. The owl was under lockdown from Gerald's shoot out and had failed to reappear. The saguaro, now holier than their mother's favorite colander, lilted at a 30-degree angle before collapsing with a SWOOSH and a THUMP, leveling the Sponge Bob pup tent.

The owl tumbled out of the hole and onto the ground. It fluttered its wings once, staggered, and then took flight, albeit in a drunken, zig zag fashion. Gerald began firing blanks at the owl, cussing as the rifle went KA SNAP, KA SNAP, KA SNAP.

Jesse wondered whether the owl flew in a lopsided fashion because it was in a daze or because it was wounded. Nevertheless, the memory of the mutilated saguaro and the wounded owl would forever live in his heart.

"Big Bang Burrito is killing everything I care about," Jesse said, finally, wondering if Tanya and Faith would ask him to elaborate. But Faith had returned her attention to her phone and Tanya yawned. She took a pull off of her vape pen.

"S...s...um...sorry," Jesse snorted, his nose more clogged than ever, first from the musty air quality, now from emotion.

"Why are you sorry?" asked Tanya.

Jesse shrugged. "For..." being such a pansy.

Tanya thought about what Jesse said. The loss of everything one cared about depressed her too, but it was inevitable, wasn't it?

"You can't stop progress." Tanya's father had always reminded her. Tanya agreed, even though corporatization was swallowing up every facet of family life and civic engagement, but it wasn't about what she or Jesse—or even what Faith...wanted, it was about what corporations wanted. It was about what people like her father—a corporate CEO himself—wanted.

You're absolutely right, Dad. I can't stop progress, but I sure as hell can have fun scaring the pants off people as I try to slow it down. Tanya took another pull from her vape pen. She shot Jesse and Faith a deadpan look. "This is what we're gonna do—"

QUACK   QUACK   QUACK   QUACK

Faith's ringtone interrupted Tanya. "Sorry, dudes. Gotta take this call," Faith answered her phone. "Hello?

".. ....?"

"This is she."

"... . .. ."

"No. No...dude, like, that can't be right...I sent you guys a payment, like a month ago—"

"... ... ., ..., ..."

"Oh...uh...really? Guess I didn't realize how quickly time flies...uh...umm...can't pay you by credit card. It's been canceled and my debit's maxed out...listen, I get paid Friday... Big Bang Burrito does direct deposit...okay?"

"....., ...?"

"Yup...sorry...just forgot...you won't send me to collections, will you?

".. ...."

"Oh, great—"

"..... ... .?"

"Yes."

"……"

"Uh-huh. Great. Thank you. Thank you—"

"…… … .. ……. .. …. … . ……?"

"Yes, bless you...you're awesome. Thanks."

Tanya grunted. "To finish what I was saying—"

"Yes, Tanya, go ahead—hey man, should we recruit more bodies? My buddies from Jittery Jo's would—"

"Forget those hipster friends of yours, Faith. Think they give two sucks about anything? They're too busy posting images of the Einkorn pancakes they had for brunch on Facebook, tweeting on Twitter and vomiting viral, or attending pickle fests with their pickle posse and having beard growing contests—"

Faith's cheeks flamed nuclear. She felt like kicking Tanya in her hairy kneecaps. "Those are my chums! By the way, they drink their beer from mason jars...."

Tanya shrugged, staring coolly at Faith. She was tempted to yank every hair out of that frizzy head of Faith's...if only to make her think clearer.

"...which means they're not only supporting small breweries, they're reusing and recycling glass jars—"

"We don't need your friends around when all we're doing is setting fire to the new BBB."

"Fire...?" Faith shot Tanya a bamboozled look.

"Setting...uh, fire...to the...b...building?" Jesse sat erect.

"We'll do it in a way that'll make it look like it was the fault of the construction crew. We could pull that off by wearing work boots to the site instead of sneakers. The police'll discover boot tracks in the sand and assume its construction workers."

Jesse stared at his lap. His legs were crossed in a way that made it appear as if he was trying to prevent a live creature from springing out from between his legs. "May I use your bathroom?" he said.

"I don't give a shit. It's to the right as you go up the stairs," said Tanya.

"Hmm..." Faith raised a brow, her forehead crinkling as if trying to solve a difficult algebraic equation. "It sounds...I don't know...like a lot of work—"

"Not really," Tanya cocked her head, listening to Jesse thud up the cellar stairs. "Maybe five minutes to...that place'll be burned to a stump in a matter of minutes." She stared at the ceiling again.

Upstairs, a toilet flushed. The sound of water rushed through the pipes, and a moment later, feet pattered down the cellar stairs.

"You seem freaked out," Tanya said to Jesse who, returning to the futon, began biting his nails.

"Well, I'm not," he stopped biting. He sat up straight.

While taking her turn on the toilet, Faith whipped out her Magic 8 Ball and gave it a good shake. Am I gonna find myself in a world of shit, if I get involved with Tanya?

Cannot Predict Now.

Faith could overhear Jesse talking to Tanya, on the other side of the bathroom door. The two were at the top of the cellar stairs when she came out of the bathroom.

"I can g...get my h...hands on m...my father and my brother's work b...boots," said Jesse.

"We're meeting at BBB, at midnight tonight." Tanya told Faith as she walked her and Jesse to the door.

"Midnight? Tonight?" Faith cocked a brow. She'd be missing Real Time With Bill Maher. Even though she could later catch it on demand. She hated to be the last one among her chums to have seen the latest episode.

"Yes, tonight. The place'll be open in less than two days. It'll be too late once it's open. It's a 24-hour restaurant...."

Faith knew this, but hadn't thought about it.

".....so, we survey the place, take notice of the vicinity...are you coming or not?"

The three were standing in the foyer, now. Faith pretended to be searching for something in her bag. The Magic 8 ball was next to her Iphone. Should I go? She shined the light from her phone onto the 8 ball, so she could see its message.

Signs point to yes.

"Sure, man, I'll bring the s'mores."

Tanya shot Faith a puzzled look. "We're just scoping the place out. Tomorrow night we do the deed. Even then, the kind of fire I'm talking about doesn't include roasting marshmallows and telling ghost stories."

Faith nodded. She would bring Hershey bars, too, just in case. Chocolate, in conjunction with the occasional dose of Adderall given to her by her friend Tim, the barista from Jittery's Jo's Java, helped motivate her.

"Don't forget flashlights," Tanya said as they stepped into the night. The air was cold as a comet trail, with an icy breeze that pricked the moist insides of Jesse's nose. The night was a beautiful one. One Jesse seldom enjoyed these days. The kind of night he remembered as a boy.

In the past, he would spend hours stargazing from the flatbed of his father's truck. Yucca's night sky had shimmered with space dust—until years later when it became deluged with light pollution. These days the domelike, yet depthless sky still maintained that same shade of lapis, and, given the cold, appeared hard and delicate as glass. Most of the stars had lost their visibility. Venus, however, appeared like a silver chip in the western sky.

"You never...uh...told us your reason for, uh, hating BBB," Jesse said to Tanya, fighting the urge to sneeze, as he and Faith made their way down the steps.

Tanya shrugged. "My reasons are irrelevant, Jesse—oh, and remember to wear dark clothes."

Barbie Versus the Incredible Hulk

Tanya's fascination with fire had begun the year she discovered her hatred for Barbie, who was beautiful while Tanya, with her silver dollar-sized port wine stain, was not—according to her mother. The birthmark wrapped itself around Tanya's chin in a perfect circle as though she'd dunked her chin in a bowl of beet juice.

One day Tanya dangled Barbie over the flame of her mother's taper candle and listened, with a twinkle in her eye, to the minute, crackling sound of the fire feeding on the synthetic fibers of Barbie's hair. The fire spoke to Tanya in a foreign language. It spoke to her in tongues. It thanked her for nourishing it.

"Poor Barbie's been scalped," Tanya cooed, inspecting the doll's hair, now curled into a kinky fray.

The chemical plastic smell, followed by the bleating of the smoke detector, caught the attention of Donna Kendrick who'd been in the kitchen yelling at Olga, her cleaning lady, for leaving stemware in the sink. Donna sniffed the air, then ran out to the dining room in time to discover her daughter clutching the mutilated doll. "You little psycho! What're you doing to my candles!?"

Scared and confused, Tanya could only blink as her mother shook her violently: "Answer me!"

When Ron Kendrick came home from Kentucky Fried Flounder's corporate headquarters, Donna sent him to Tanya's room to ask her why she'd been playing with the candles. Tanya shrugged as she held Boomer, her stuffed dog, to her chest. At first, she thought her anger was solely directed at Mother for having exchanged the Incredible Hulk lunch box that Olga had bought her for a Barbie lunchbox. However, when Daddy stepped into her room to have a word with her—he was so tall, his head nearly brushed the top of the door frame—she realized that the angry floppies in her stomach also had to do with the fact that she saw so little of him. He was a large, large man, yet he occupied such a small, small part of her life. It seemed he'd rather spend all his time with his business than be with her—and she noticed that Mother seemed to be yelling more these days—and crying too. Tanya had to wonder if this was because Daddy had become such a small, small part of her life, too. Setting things on fire helped Tanya to feel calm, but she couldn't tell Daddy this. He might get mad and stop loving her.

"Okay, kiddo, I'll step out so you can have some thinking time. Mom says you're to stay up here `til she tells you to come down."

As far as Tanya was concerned, being made to stay in her room was like being in a pink-walled jail cell, complete with a Barbie-themed, lace canopy Mother bought her for Christmas. "Green is not for girls," Mother snorted when Tanya had begged to have her walls painted pea green like the Incredible Hulk. She loved the Incredible Hulk.

On the day the painters came, Tanya had locked herself in the downstairs bathroom, off the kitchen, while Mother had been upstairs telling the painters how many coats of pink Tanya's bedroom walls needed. Tanya felt an ache in her throat but had refused to cry. Instead, she'd held Mother's favorite doily over the sink and set it on fire.

After her father had finished talking to her, and had left the room, Tanya sat at the top of the hallway stairs, staring at the tops of her parents' heads. The second floor railing cast bar-like shadows on her Barbie pajamas—which she'd puked on once, after having eaten the "Bean Me Up Scotty."

Mother and Daddy were sitting at the big dining table. Olga was lighting the tall, skinny candles while Daddy struggled to open a bottle of his favorite drink. Tanya smiled lovingly at him, noticing that while he seemed so important whenever he sat at his big, shiny desk and talked to people on phones all day—she knew this from having spent the occasional evening hanging around his office—he wasn't the type who could do stuff with his hands.

"She won't talk," Daddy told Mother in that scaredy cat voice he used around her.

"Great. First she's playing with fire and now she's being a little brat by ignoring us when we ask her a question." Mother's face was reflected in the table's shiny surface. Her nostrils were flaring. They always did that whenever she didn't approve of something. They made her look like Carl— the cranky colt Tanya had been forced to ride at summer horse camp.

"Don't even think about bringing that upstairs," Donna barked at Olga, who—a moment ago had been spooning her famous homemade ravioli onto a plastic Barbie plate—froze during mid-scoop, her pale face going stone gray.

The smell of tangy tomato sauce, layered between pillows of ricotta cheese, had drifted up the stairs. The smell made Tanya's stomach growl. She was ready to talk.

"I wanted to give Barbie a haircut," Tanya lied. "But I couldn't find the scissors, so I dunked her head in the candle."

Donna thought she'd teach Tanya a lesson about playing with fire by throwing her stuffed dog in the fireplace. She'd been waiting for an excuse. Ron had won it for Tanya at the fair. The thing was ugly.

Tanya watched Boomer's polka dotted body and his button eyes, frozen in perpetual surprise, ignite. Almost instantly, he became a pile of ash. It wasn't the first time she'd seen Mother throw things into the fireplace. She'd often burn things she felt she had no use for: the pot holders Auntie Celia made for her, "They don't match my kitchen walls and they look homemade;" a pair of socks Auntie Celia gave her, "I refuse to wear rayon ever again. We grew up poor, but Auntie Celia still acts like we're poor;" and the photos of herself as a teenager, with terrible acne, to name a few.

Tanya refused to cry over Boomer. Instead, she stared at Mother until Mother's nose stopped flaring and she nervously pulled her gaze away. "Finish your food and go to bed, Tanya."

After Mother had left the room, Tanya scowled down at Barbie who lay on the rug, next to the chair where Tanya had dropped her. Despite the scorched hair Barbie still had that unwavering, bleached smile and that vapid, blue-eyed gaze, which seemed to mock Tanya.

Tanya swallowed the last bite of food before bringing her slippered foot down on Barbie's head. She then vowed to herself that she'd never play with fire again. She would, instead, return to her other favorite pastime: sticking forks in light sockets.

Hindsight is 20/20

Faith stood guard behind a boulder, sweating inside her ape suit. Yawning, she dreamed about flannel pajamas and chocolate-covered pretzels while Tanya, also clad in an ape suit, jimmied the metal box mounted on the rear wall of Big Bang Burrito.

An earworm of the Mission Impossible theme song played in Tanya's head as she smashed the GSM chip with her crowbar, in order to prevent the security alarm from going off. Earlier, she noticed that there was no cop cruiser on duty when she, along with Jesse and Faith, walked past the restaurant's parking lot—not that police presence would have made a difference, since Yucca's officers were known to coop during their graveyard shift.

"Isn't there...uh...gonna be a ton of...uh...cops out tonight? Being that it's Mischief Night?" Jesse had asked.

"Young people are too cool for Mischief Night. They'd rather play video games than egg houses...if there're any eggers at all, the cops'll be too busy busting `em to bother with us."

"What if we do...um...encounter a cop and...uh...he, uh...asks what we're up to?"

"Tell `im we're going to a Halloween party," Tanya had snorted.

"How long's this gonna take?" asked Faith.

"Will you two quit bugging me with questions?"

Tanya kicked down the back door. She hunted down the surveillance cameras. She dashed about the restaurant, stuffing wads of Quilted Northern into the eyeballs of Big Brother. One such eyeball lurked in the corner, suspended high above the cash register. It was probably not yet activated, but she was not about to take chances. She waved a furry paw, beckoning Jesse, who had been hiding behind the drive through menu, to follow her into the building.

The chemical smell of brand spanking newness overwhelmed Jesse's nostrils when he entered. The place reeked of vinyl, sawdust and fresh paint. That aside, it was no different from any of the other Big Bang Burrito restaurants. Each had a mural, covering one whole wall, that depicted the Sonoran Desert in a culturally cliched way: mesas, donkeys, sombreros and chili-peppers. All had seating areas with orange plastic booths and mustard-yellow tabletops.

Tanya removed her mask. She swiveled her flashlight toward the ceiling, letting its beam rest on a silver gadget attached to a thin pipe. It resembled a garden spigot. There were several such gadgets that comprised the sprinkler system.

"Uh-huh." A menacing smile spread on Tanya's lips as she followed the pipe along the ceiling with the beam of her flashlight. The back of her ape costume blended into the shadows, and soon all Jesse could see was the back of her rust-colored hair. When asked, "Why the costumes?" Tanya had answered, "It's better for people to report Big Foot sightings than vandals."

Jesse hung out by the service counter, under the surveillance camera, now blinded by TP. He was left in the dark and the silence, and it made him nervous. To circumvent this, he whistled a tune with no melody, imagining what 36 hours from now might look like. Employees would stand right where he stood, under the brash LED lighting. Construction workers, men like his brother and father, would filter in come lunch time.

Jesse could picture Bruce ordering his favorite: the "Bean Me Up Scottie," a chimichanga stuffed with wild boar trimmings and frozen beans that were fried whole, mashed and then refried again—and smothered in tangy Area 51 Rocket Sauce. He tried not to think about Bruce or meat trimmings and was relieved when Faith finally appeared.

She paused at the counter, opposite Jesse, and began flicking her flashlight off and on, off and on, off and on. She thought about Big Bang Burrito and the shift that lay ahead: sweating in her brown polyester work shirt, with the head of a space alien on its lapel, her scalp itchy under her orange visor. Her feet would be sweaty and sore from standing at the pickup window for hours, ringing in orders placed by mothers and their kids, all screaming for the nine-piece poo poo platter. The platter consisted of three pinto bean popovers, three roadrunner nuggets and three racing strips served with: Atomic Sweet 'n Sour Sauce or Roswell Kool Rancher's. Faith would leave the restaurant at the end of her shift exhausted, with the scent of refried beans clinging to her hair.

Big Bang Burrito aired its commercials on the radio every morning. Faith had often heard it on her drive to work: "Start your day with a bang at Big Bang Burrito!" The slogan had begun to grate on Faith, but with rent due she was beginning to hear a whole other slogan, one with the potential for being more than grating: "Start your day with an eviction notice!" and wondered if she had done the right thing by blowing off work—hindsight is 20/20.

Jesse amused himself by making shadow puppets on the wall above the hand washing sink. His testicles turned to icicles inside his boxers, however, when a scorpion skittered into the pale circle of light emitting from the end of his flashlight. He was convinced that these part-shrimp, part-lobster creatures were not of planet Earth.

The scorpion shimmied down the wall, its stinger raised, ready to lance any jackass who dared fuck with it. Jesse felt his knees quake from fear. They threatened to liquify out from under him. A warm wetness bloomed in the crotch of his boxers and threatened to soak through the ape fur. Jesse's face flushed nuclear. He was thankful for the dark.

Faith had removed her ape mask and was now texting in one of the orange booths. Her phone cast a blue glow on her pallid face, which reflected in the window facing the parking lot.

A shape moved from the corner of Jesse's vision. It blended in with the blackness of the unlit kitchen entryway, then detached itself from the shadows and moved toward him. Jesse threw his paws up in defense, backing himself into the counter, but it was only Tanya in her ape costume.

"There'e two things about this place. First, it's a tinderbox...the walls are built from cheap particle board. Two, it's far from the fire station...what's the matter?"

"I uh, um...uh...have ta...uh, leave."

"Oh." Tanya's business-like tone wilted.

"I just pi...uh...I uh...got a nature call...uh, emergency call—"

"When you gotta go, you gotta go."

Jesse could not agree more with this adage. "Sorry if I—"

"What are you doing?!' Tanya hissed at Faith, whose bewildered eyes locked on Tanya's. "Get the fuck away from that window! You wanna get us busted?"

"Wow, man. Chill out...I was looking for a job on Craig's List. I'd heard that Kentucky Fried Flounder was hiring—"

"Why aren't you outside standing guard?"

"I was cold. And I thought—"

"Hello...?" Faith answered her phone, her thin voice echoing off the ceiling. "Hello?"

"... . ..., ...?"

"Who's this?"

".. ...., ..."

"What survey? Sorry, don't remember filling out a survey—"

"... ... ."

"What...?...What...?...Can you hear me now...?!" Faith inched toward Tanya who began drumming her fingers on the service counter. "Yeah...okay...now I remember...yes...I donated a dollar to your cause...yes...I'm still all about saving the Aardvarks—"

"..... ... .?"

"Oh...now you want a dollar to save the sloths? Oh...you know I'd love to...but like...I need to save myself." Faith hung up. She smiled sweetly at Tanya. "You were saying?"

Who Needs the Wilderness?

From the driveway, Jesse could see silver light strobing in the living room window, and two brawny silhouettes. The silver light, coming from the Timorlans' enormous flat screen T.V., was a reminder to Jesse that it was Thursday night—Gerald and Shep night—a fun-filled night of cursing, grunting and beer guzzling that would go until four a.m. There would be pizza and there would be video games—but Jesse would never be invited.

Sighing, Jesse paused outside the door to peel off the ape costume. He hung it over the rail to dry. He tied his hoodie around his non-existent hips in order to conceal the evidence of his embarrassing moment before going inside. A wall of digital sound assaulted him the moment he slipped indoors. Audience cheers, mingled with sounds of virtual violence and male one-upmanship: THWAK!! SPLOOP!! OOOOF!! drilled Jesse's ears. The boys were playing WW All Stars, Gerald's favorite.

DING!! DING!! DING!! DING!! tolled the wrestling bell.

"Take that, ya punk!!" Shep spat, wielding his thumbs over the gameboy's buttons in order to get his opponent into a headlock.

"No way, Dude!" Gerald snarled through clenched teeth, his muscles sprang from his biceps as his thumbs worked the gameboy. "You suuuck!!" Jesse couldn't tell if Gerald's insult was directed at his virtual opponent or Shep or both.

"Argghhh, Fuck!" Gerald slammed the gameboy down on the coffee table as Randy Savage flopped face down in the ring. "This game sucks anyway." He sipped from his can of Bud Ice while Jesse practically tripped over his own two feet trying to run past, but only made it as far as the couch when the hoodie slid off and pooled at his feet.

"Hey, Jessica? What's with the land mine on the back of your ass?"

"Uh...I...land m...mine?" Jesse ducked behind the Jade plant, fumbling as he retied the hoody.

"Dude," Gerald snapped his fingers, something he did when trying to make a point. "I'm talking about the stain on the back of your ass!"

"I...uh...um...sat in a puddle." It was a crummy lie since not a single drop of rain had fallen on Yucca in nearly three years.

"I hear BJs is having a sale on Pampers." Gerald wiped the beer foam from his mustache.

Jesse slammed his bedroom door. He peeled off his wet boxers, wishing that his brother would move out. With his 29th birthday approaching, the move for Gerald was long overdue.

"I wish the jerk was dead," Jesse murmured, throwing back his comforter.

A coffee table book, borrowed from the library, tumbled to the floor: A History of Cholla County. Earlier, he'd been admiring the book's black-and-white photos of Yucca from the 1940s to the 1960s, when there existed nothing but desert prairie filled with grass that undulated in the wind like seaweed waving from the bottom of a creek bed, frozen in permanent motion on film.

The photos made him think of wide-open-spaces, which made him think about Clyde Chestnut Barrow and Bonnie Parker, speeding along the dirt roads in a stolen Ford V8—detouring across the lovely empty landscape with the law on their heels.

Jesse had tried to imagine himself as a modern day Clyde, escaping in his mother's Honda Fit after lifting an algebra text from a Barnes & Noble, but couldn't. At best, he'd leave a doozy of a scratch on Mom's paint job from sideswiping parked cars. At worst, he'd leave a trail of human road lasagna in his wake. Damage would be done to the Fit's undersides from ramming into curbs or running over soccer moms and little old ladies with shopping carts filled with Fresh Step kitty litter.

By the time the cops caught up with him, he'd be scraping Granny guts from the grooves of his mother's Good Year tires, or ditching the Fit behind the IMAX theater, or holding a stick up in the Trader Joe's snack isle, forcing all shoppers to fork over their salted caramels. I'd've gotten away if it wasn't for this sprawl! He'd imagined himself telling the cops while being handcuffed and taken away.

And I'd have done fine if it hadn't been for that scorpion. Jesse allowed himself to dissolve into the pillows—he wished they'd swallow him whole. Tears slid down his cheeks, soaking the starched pillowcases, patterned with sheep playing the fiddle.

Not certain if saving the planet was worth the fear and humiliation, and beginning to wonder if the destruction of the natural world was inevitable, Jesse began to think harder about the question posed in Edward Abbey's book: "Wilderness, who needs it?"

Agent Freddy

Autumn frost twinkled on the sun-baked grass outside the post office. The smell of sage mingled with the nippy morning air. The nip burned the inside of Tanya's nose as she trundled up the steps, noting that the sage scent was rare and that the good graces of a frost always seemed to push the air pollution down—for a few hours anyway.

She wasn't sure if she should expect anything or not as she unlocked the P.O. box, since, aside from bills, she seldom received anything except Big Bang Burrito and Kentucky Fried Flounder coupons—and Harriet Carter catalogues, which sold petroleum-based gadgets such as puppy dog motion detectors and slipper warmers.

Thinking that they'd be nice for those cold January mornings, Tanya had made the mistake of ordering the slipper warmers, which consisted of inserts that went inside a pair of slippers. The miniature heating pads were sewn into the lining of the inserts, and were powered by tiny A76 batteries. Tanya'd had the slipper warmers for only a week when the heating pads began to overheat. Her big toes felt as if they were on fire, and she'd begun to wonder if her feet were experiencing what middle-aged women call hot flashes—until the pads crapped out altogether. The slipper warmers were then donated to the landfill. Harriet Carter hasn't stopped sending Tanya catalogues since.

As predicted, the coupons were there. No Harriet Carter this time, thank God. While peering into the otherwise empty post office box, a colic sensation filled Tanya's sternum as she tried to convince herself that Daddy did care, but was too busy to send her a birthday card this year, and that she should check her Facebook messages before flying into a homicidal rage. A smiley face emoji, accompanied by a quick two-liner on Facebook, was his usual mode of communication—even though the last one he'd sent her was from six months ago. His communication style had gotten worse, ever since Tanya decided to boycott all financial assistance from him, concluding a fight they'd had over the fact that he'd re-married.

I see more of the man's corporation than the man himself. Tanya tossed the Kentucky Fried Flounder coupons into the recycling bin. She took a deep breath, trying not to let her expectations of how a father ought to act disrupt the euphoric mental state she'd felt upon waking, and continued to enjoy until now.

The euphoria she always experienced before pulling one of her "stunts" came with a profound alertness and an extreme enhancement of the senses. The Dupont stain-resistant curtains, which framed her basement window, were normally hunter green. Today they looked like a nuclear shade of teal, especially when the morning sun bled through them. The synthetic floral scent of Bounce fabric softener, lingering in Ginger's dryer, had overwhelmed her nose. She could even hear the beating of wings of the fruit flies as they floated mindlessly over a honey-vanilla tea bag that'd welded itself to the inside of her coffee mug. It was like listening to the string section in Beethoven's "Flight of the Bumblebee."

Though she could perceive the world at a microscopic level during times of mania, there seemed to be no words in the lexicon to describe the way that her actions seemed to move at the speed of light—before her ability to reason could catch up with them.

Without these "stunts" and the euphoria that preceded them, she felt dead inside. They were a reason to exist, and she could always count on them being a hoot. Tonight's shenanigans would be no exception. They were going to be magnificent. Although she did feel an inkling of reservation concerning her two sidekicks: Flighty Faith and Jumpy Jesse. Tanya the Terrible, as she coined herself, had always carried out tasks alone—always. Jesse always seemed as startled stiff as the plastic reindeer ornaments Aunt Celia kept in the yard—until way past Christmas.

But the interactions with Faith and Jesse made her realize how dehydrated she was for companionship.

***

With a shaky hand, Ginger yanked the ball chain. The creases in her forehead deepened when the light to the cellar stairwell refused to flick on. *Why on God's blue planet didn't Tanya tell me about the burned-out bulb? Or just change the damn thing herself? Kids these days have no mind to do anything for themselves!*

Tottering in her slippers, Ginger clutched the rail. The thunk of her cane punctuated each step as she bumped along, slowly descending into the dank depths of the old house. The steps were steep and they made her joints pop deep inside her boney knees.

The cellar still scared the living turkey gizzards out of her. One time, about a year ago, she came down to do laundry and found a homeless man sleeping behind her water heater. She figured he must've sneaked in through the outside hatch to the cellar. The hatch was in disrepair. But once it was repaired, the potential threat became the idea that she might fall and break a bone and not be able to get to her operator relay service. She had two such devices. One in the living room, next to her La-Z-Boy, the other on her nightstand—both light-years from her reach. Should anyone drop by to check on her....? She wouldn't know because she wouldn't hear them knocking or entering. She'd remain in that cellar for days before anyone ever found her. The threat of becoming marooned in the bowels of her own home faded considerably, however, when Tanya, her new housemate, took up residence a month ago.

Today, unfortunately, Ginger would need to invade Tanya's lair in order to locate her wayward cat, believed to be exploring its damp, dank reaches. At the landing, she paused to catch her breath and to let her eyes adjust to the dark, but the shadows threatened to snuff out her vision. Mildew and the residual spicy scent of that funny little device Tanya liked to suck on tickled Ginger's nose as she inched forward—she never gave Tanya hell about vaping indoors because the smell brought fond memories of her late husband who'd died from smoking ten years earlier.

A finger of sunlight seeped in from Tanya's high rectangular window. Ginger groped for the light switch, behind a giant tapestry with a bust of Che Guevara. Her eyes bugged under the intensity of the LED overhead lights.

She pursed her lips in a kissing gesture, in an attempt at making smoochy sounds cats will often answer to. She began to wonder what her voice sounded like to Freddy—or if he could hear her at all—when a pair of round yellow eyes emerged from the blackness of Tanya's armoire. Its doors had been left ajar.

Freddy was sprawled lazily on a small stack of newspapers, his furry bulk half-hidden under the hem of a pea coat. Ginger felt a subtle vibration under her hand when she patted him, and knew he was purring. He squirmed under her grasp when she tried to lift him into her arms. He promptly returned to the newspaper stack.

"Wasss the madder Fre...d?" He needed to find contentment in her room, not Tanya's. When she tried to lift him again he swatted her.

"Fre...dy! Min' me now!"

As if to apologize, Freddy dutifully stepped out of the armoire, rubbed lovingly against Ginger's slippered foot, but then dove back in and began rubbing against the newspapers. He sprang from Ginger's arms when she reached for him again, then ducked deeper into the armoire.

Damn it, cat! You're giving my heart a workout.

Freddy wasn't trying to be difficult, he was trying to warn Mistress about the impending doom, which hadn't been his intent when he first wandered into this shadowy place. The wandering began with a craving to explore, for Freddy's life as a house cat had become rote. Sneaking outdoors was not an option, however. He'd decided this after having spent enough afternoons observing the hulking objects that sped past his house, from the safety of the window sill. The objects weren't animals and they weren't human, but they held humans inside of them and took humans places. Freddy learned this from all the times Mistress had put him inside of one, so that they could visit the man in the white coat—the one who had put an end to his humping career.

Those hulking objects were deadly. He couldn't outrun them, but they could flatten him the way Mistress' rolling pin could flatten a pie crust. No matter, it was better to remain indoors where he could keep an eye on Mistress—especially now that that girl was living with them, whom he didn't trust any further than he could spray.

He'd felt a hiss building in his throat from the moment he and the girl became acquainted. He'd meant to be polite when she leaned over to pet him. Instead, he arched his back, spit at her and then slithered under the La-Z-Boy. She had a funny mark on her chin and she smelled bad. It was something in her sweat. It was sour and rang of danger, of evil. It made his fur crawl.

Moreover, he understood from the time he was a kitten that Mistress was different from other humans. Sounds were something he heard and responded to all of the time, while

Mistress didn't respond to them at all. Of course, he had big ears and could hear everything, including the mice rustling in the walls.

One time he hopped on the window ledge to sunbathe and accidentally knocked Mistress' plant to the floor. The pot shattered, making an awful noise that made Freddy curl his tail in shame. Mistress had been at the sink drying dishes and had not so much as looked up.

Once, when it was raining hard, Freddy saw jangles of light zigzag across the sky and hid behind the La-Z-Boy, panting from anxiety over the booming and the rumbling that'd followed while Mistress never moved from the chair. She continued to read one of those thick, paper things by the fire.

And Mistress never seemed to notice when the girl entered the room, until the girl sneaked up behind her, the way he would sneak up behind a mouse. Freddy pounced on mice, killed them and ate them all the time. Would the girl one day do the same to Mistress?

Nevertheless, Freddy hadn't expected his wandering to end with his detecting a funny odor coming from the hole he'd climbed into, an odor that didn't belong in a place where humans hung their fur.

When Freddy began to knead the stack of newspapers, Ginger realized that he was trying to show her something. She leaned her cane against the armoire as Freddy hopped out and then flopped down beside her. Her joints creaked as she reached inside the armoire, which she swore smelled vaguely of gasoline, and pulled the first newspaper off of the stack. Its front pages were flipped to the C section. The police log was highlighted in yellow marker:

11:00 p.m. a woman on Petrified Forrest Lane
reported a trash fire behind Piggly Wiggly.

Ginger shrugged. She put the newspaper back on the stack and started to get up, but Freddy sank his claws into the meatiest part of her calf. She realized then, that it was her duty to glance at the next paper:

Yucca Resident Accused of Fraud Following Garage Fire.

Freddy purred as he rolled onto his side and began drooling while kneading Ginger's calf. Ginger took the third paper from the stack. Its cover was graced with two photos. The first was of the now defunct Horde & Stuff self-storage center. The second photo was of the same self-storage center engulfed in flames:

Ape-like Creature Flees the Scene of Five Alarm Blaze.

Ginger pulled the fourth paper from the stack:

Mystery Fires and Big Foot Sightings Leave Yucca's
Residents On Edge.

Ginger scratched the mole on her chin as she read the fourth paper's front page. She herself hadn't been aware of any fires, except for the one at Yucca's Church of Christ where she and her friends attended Sunday services. But that one didn't count, as it was a controlled brush fire, albeit a huge, barely controlled brush fire which Tanya had volunteered to man as part of the church grounds maintenance crew.

All 15 papers in Tanya's stack contained articles about Cholla's mystery fires. Not knowing what to make of them, Ginger tried to arrange the papers in the order that she found them, but the top two slid off of the pile. She became more aware of the gasoline smell as she poked her head inside the armoire. Her fingers scraped something plastic and cool to the touch as she reached for the papers that'd fallen. She peered under the pea coat and discovered a gasoline jug.

Jimminy shit crickets! Damned kid...doesn't she have any sense?

The day that Tanya manned the church brushfire suddenly appeared in Ginger's memory: the gleam in Tanya's eyes when the other grounds keepers had hollered at her not to add any more debris to the fire, and how she'd refused to listen: "What safety code?" She'd shrugged, a mad grin on her lips. Only when the fire truck arrived did Tanya stop adding to the fire, but even as the firemen gave her a good scolding, not once did Tanya appear remorseful.

The gas jug was empty. This did not bring Ginger comfort, however, as this wasn't really about lack of common sense— so much as realizing, in a moment's flash, that she could very well be residing with the firebug of Cholla County. The "Bean Me Up Scotty" that Ginger had eaten for breakfast didn't sit well in her stomach.

The Living Dead

Faith stood at the mirror, swiping Oxy pads over a cluster of PMS pimples. Bloated, fatigued and just plain down on herself, she pondered whether or not she had the oomph to parade around town—to vandalize buildings in an ape suit with her compatriots at two in the a.m.

She grabbed her Magic 8 Ball from off the top of the refrigerator. "Should I bail?" she asked, giving it a shake.

Reply hazy, try again.

In a half hour, Tanya and Jesse would be picking her up in the car Tanya planned to borrow, but the salted carmel Froyo and Turner Classic Movies were waiting for Faith. Tonight's two a.m. feature, Night of the Living Dead, was a favorite of hers. She flipped on the tube. The clock on the screen read 1:50 a.m., which meant Faith had exactly nine minutes and 30 seconds to change into her ape costume. I feel so fat in that thing! She spooned Froyo from the carton and into her mouth, believing that one or two or several bites of frozen sweetness would help motivate her toward the greater good of society.

***

As usual, the door to Ginger's bedroom was open. Tanya, adorning her ape costume, loitered in the hallway, watching the sleeping bodies of Freddy and Ginger, who was knocked off in a coma, her cheeks sunken. They reminded Tanya of two deflated balloons. Tanya couldn't help but see Ginger as nothing more than a cadaver, sleeping soundlessly in that silver street light that crept in through the blinds from the nearby plaza. This was good news for Tanya, who planned to take off in Ginger's sedan—which Ginger could no longer drive. The car got its use whenever Tanya chauffeured Ginger to church, the supermarket and doctor appointments. Tanya felt certain that Ginger would say yes, if she'd asked to borrow the car, but what fun was there in having permission?

Freddy lay at the foot of Ginger's bed, curled into a black velvety donut, catnapping as cats do, his eyes ready to flick open at the slightest sound or movement—a living, breathing, motion detector ready to pounce. The girl was there. He knew it even before his eyes flicked open. He could smell that sour smell of hers, even while in a doze and dreaming of dancing sardines.

Tanya brushed against the flimsy wood of the door. The door creaked. Freddy's ears pricked. He rose, stared at the doorway. His fur bristled at what he saw: a black furry face. Was it another cat? Whatever it was, it was far bigger than he was and it was staring him down.

Ginger's eyes fluttered open when she felt Freddy stir. A black and furry figure, the size of a small man, was skulking outside her bedroom door. However, her brain was too sleep-logged from the Lunesta she'd ingested for her to register that she ought to be terrified. It was when Freddy stood keen and erect, like a miniature panther guarding his kingdom, his eyes laser beamed on the figure, his back arched and his ears back—that she suddenly felt wide awake.

Jimminy shit Crickets! An ape! Ginger's lips curled into a horrified capital O, but the terror was so great it paralyzed her vocal chords. She couldn't even draw in enough air to scream. And so she lay on the mattress like a slab of defenseless marble.

Freddy hissed. Tanya slipped away. Ginger lay like a wax dummy. Freddy leapt off the bed. Ginger clapped a hand to her chest. Tanya tiptoed down the hall. Freddy followed.

Jimminy shit Crickets! Ginger tumbled out of bed and grabbed her cane, finally. She hobbled after Freddy. Freddy trotted after Tanya. Tanya tiptoed through the kitchen.

In the glow of the stove's hood light, Ginger could see the ape, who, seemingly unaware of Ginger, slipped out the back. It slammed the door in Freddy's face on its way out. Ginger scooped up the cat, felt his little heart thrum under his fur even as he tried to squirm from her grasp.

From the kitchen window, Ginger spotted the ape getting away in her sedan. Still clutching Freddy, she hobbled toward the cellar door. She must alert Tanya about the break in.

***

Faith's spoon went CLANG as she tossed it, along with the empty Froyo container, into the kitchen sink piled with dirty dishes.

She blamed her laziness on gluten sensitivity. In the waiting room, at the gynecologist's, she'd read a two-page article by Dr. Oz, which had graced the glossy pages of O, The Oprah Magazine. She'd learned that gluten intolerance may be linked to indecisiveness and lack of ambition. Thus, she began a crusade against products containing gluten, which had lasted all of two days when she discovered that Turkey Lurkey Jerky, her favorite snack, had gluten in it. A life without Turkey Lurkey Jerky was no life at all.

It was 2:20 a.m. and Night of the Living Dead had started and Faith was so sucked into the scene where Johnny teases his sister in the cemetery, that she barely heard her phone ring:

QUACK   QUACK   QUACK QUACK

"What's up?" Faith asked, eyes glued to the TV. "Can you hold on a second?" She didn't want to miss the part where Johnny and the zombie get into a tussle.

"We're here! Are you fucking coming or not!" Tanya barked. Faith groaned. Should I bother? She shook the Magic 8 ball:

As I see it, yes.

"Hi, Tanya. Can you come back in an hour? I'll be dressed and ready by then." Faith couldn't even remember where she put the ape costume.

Silence on the other end.

"Tanya? Are you there?

Silence.

"Hello?" Faith glanced at the phone's screen.

Call ended.

Faith did plan on going, really she did, she just...hadn't realized how important this was to Tanya or to Jesse. Changing one's mind at the last minute, not following through on things, or just plumb forgetting about the day in front of her didn't seem all that strange to Faith. The credo "whatever will be, will be" is one she'd acquired over the years through growing up with the music of Doris Day and a delinquent dad and a malfunctioning mom—who kept a small, plastic cache at her bedside table. It was labeled M, T, W, Th, F, S, S and contained two kinds of pills that'd reminded young Faith of Good & Plenty candies. The white ones made Mother sleep on the couch all day, while the pink ones made her extremely jumpy and super happy.

Sleepy Mother ignored Faith and Eileen while watching television for hours. Peppy Mother bounced from job to job, thus causing the family to move from town to town and later state to state. Under the influence of the pink Good & Plenties, Mother took on many creative interests. Oh, she had lots of them: making tie-dye T-shirts in the bath tub, reupholstering brand new furniture, crocheting sock monkeys... their apartment would be cluttered with half-finished sock monkeys. Monkeys missing arms, monkeys missing eyes. Monkeys missing a leg or two.

Though perplexing, none of these oddities were as bad as the times when Mother would forget to show up for Faith's dance recitals. Clad in her crinoline skirt and leotard, Faith would scan the audience, trying to locate Mother's rotund face among the sea of faces, with no success.

One time, Faith received a thunderous ovation for her dance solo. Yet after the curtain came down, the other dancers were greeted by their mothers, brandishing flower bouquets, while Faith was greeted by her dance coach, sans flowers, who then had to carpool her home. Only then did Mother's odd behavior become a bonafide let down. Only then, did Faith begin to associate accomplishment with pain.

The Prickly Beast

"It's just you and me now," Tanya told Jesse as they joggled down Turkey Buzzard Road, a dry and dusty strip, sparsely settled by sagging motor homes on cinder blocks. Jesse knew the route well. Its first quarter mile lay 200 yards beyond Big Bang Burrito's parking lot, before continuing into the hills where it eventually came to a fork: the left leading to the town dump and ending at a land mine, the right circling back into town. It was one of the few country roads left within Yucca's town limits, a wasteland cluttered with the skeletal remains of junked cars.

The night lay heavy around them. Unable to see anything ahead, beyond the reaches of the sedan's headlights, Jesse turned his gaze to the passenger's side window. The glowing eyes of kangaroo rats peered at him from behind mesquite bushes on the side of the road. In the distance, he saw a cluster of shimmering neon dots comprising Yucca's downtown.

Jesse pointed a finger at the pull out, next to an outcropping of boulders. He informed Tanya of the parking spot behind them, but warned her to avoid the wash-out. Once behind the boulder, Tanya got the notion to drive into the wash-out anyway. It merged with a dried-up creek bed, which formed a high ravine, which would better conceal the car from anyone who happened to drive by.

"Where are we going?" Jesse whined.

"Shhh…I gotta concentrate." Tanya killed the engine and shifted the car into neutral, allowing it to roll into the creek bed.

While waiting for Tanya to give further instructions, Jesse squeezed his loins. *You are not gonna pee your ape suit.* He'd never done anything illegal in his life, except smoke pot with Tony the bagger while on lunch break when he'd worked at the Piggly Wiggly. Oh…and one time he stole a shopping cart to use as a laundry basket…and once he stole hisneighbor's keep-off-the-grass sign. Okay, so that made three illegal things, he noted when he saw the sign up ahead:

PRIVATE PROPERTY
NO TRESPASSING
VIOLATORS WILL BE PROSECUTED

"Uh...Tanya?"

"Yeah, Jesse." Impatience rang in Tanya's voice as she lifted the last gasoline jug out of the trunk.

"Do you, um...uh, think this'll work?"

"Of course it'll work. It'll be tremendous." Tanya pulled on her ape mask. She locked the door. Jesse did the same. They trundled up the bank of the dusty ravine, gas jugs in tow. Panting from exertion, Jesse stared out at what was left of his beloved whiffle ball field—once they reached the top—at the remaining bit of field not tarred over. Big Bang Burrito lay 200 hundred yards away. It would be a ten-minute romp through the field to get there, give or take...or so he guessed.

"All we need to do is douse the area around the gas grill and the fryolator, and then run like hell. The place'll be reduced to a lump of coal by the time that first fire truck even arrives—if we carry this out efficiently. The police station is on the other side of town, so we'll be back in the car, changed out of our ape gear and on the road before the cops even arrive. After, we'll stop at Apple Bees where we can relax, drink a shake and have a burger. Sound good?"

***

Ginger entered Tanya's room. There was an indentation on the futon where Tanya had been sleeping, but no Tanya.

Jimminy shit Crickets! Could Tanya have shapeshifted into an ape? Ginger was then reminded of the news articles about fires and ape sightings and of the gas jug inside of Tanya's armoire. Ginger thumped her way up the stairs to dial the police from her operator relay service, glad that her sedan had a GPS tracking system.

***

Gerald was an insomniac. As usual, he couldn't sleep. But rather than waste time trying, he slipped out to the garage to complete a project he'd started: stripping and refinishing a coffee table in the shape of a naked woman. His brush lay under the table. When reaching for his brush, he noticed that a nail was loose in one of the table's leg joints.

The hammer would be in his tool bag, only he couldn't find the tool bag in its usual spot: the third shelf of the tool crib.

He searched his father's work truck to no avail. He realized then that he'd left it at the worksite. The last time he remembered seeing it was when he sat in the shade of the saguaro where he and his father had eaten their lunch.

But his own forgetfulness wasn't his fault. It was that of his co-worker, Pat, who'd distracted him while on the job site by working him into a tizzy over politics. Gerald had been nonplussed and nearly choked on his bologna sandwich when he discovered that Pat had been a Hillary supporter—and then became indignant. His father had had to step in for the third time in one month to defuse a potential fist fight between the two men—after Pat threatened to file a harassment charge against Gerald for calling him a snowflake.

The tool bag was worth thousands of dollars, and Gerald's job at Big Bang Burrito was complete—other contractors had been hired to do the job of removing the saguaro and erecting the neon sign. The workers would be there in the morning, while he and his father began another job: erecting a luxury condo on the other side of town.

Gerald got in the van. He glanced in the direction of Jesse's bedroom window as he was pulling out of the driveway. For a change the window was dark. At this hour, the kid was usually in his room, reading, but earlier had left the house wearing an ape costume.

*He's probably bobbing for apples at some heavily chaperoned, lame-ass Halloween party for babies...*although Gerald did find it odd that his bookworm-of-a-brother should attend a party in the middle of the night.

***

Tanya and Jesse jimmied their way through the back door of Big Bang Burrito. As before, Tanya blinded the cameras with toilet tissue. Jesse bumbled after her, practically on her heels as she crept toward the kitchen. She stopped abruptly and he smacked into her. The gasoline swished violently inside the jugs.

"Watch for any cars that might pull in," Tanya told him, grabbing his jug and disappearing into the kitchen.

Jesse fidgeted at the counter, his heart thumping in his ears, his knees quaking as he kept his eyes peeled on the parking lot. From his post he could hear the sounds of liquid leaving the jugs: GLUG, GLUG, GLUG and spilling onto the floor: SPLISH, SPLASH, SPLUSH. The sounds were enough to make him hurl. Surprisingly, he had not yet pissed himself. Perhaps this was because tonight's shenanigans, thus far, had already scared the piss out of him.

Having given the fryolator an extra douse, Tanya shined her flashlight on the red-tiled floor, making sure that the gasoline puddles were where she needed them to be. She then inspected her ape costume to be sure she hadn't spilled any on herself. That'd be a disaster.

She struck a match. She dropped it in the puddle around the fryolator and grinned when a four foot flame sprang from the floor—then another, then another, then another. A row of yellow-orange flames danced into action like a fountain of fire that'd been activated, causing a fantastic light show in Big Bang Burrito's brand-new kitchen. With the walls all aglow, Tanya felt as if she was on the inside of a Jack-o'-lantern—inside of a tandoor oven. She dashed out to the counter. "Let's go!"

Jesse hesitated long enough to see the thermal nuclear tongues leap from the kitchen archway before rushing over the floor tiles, where he'd stood a moment ago. The tongues morphed into one unified wave, making a crackling, airy SWOOSH as they devoured the countertop.

The heat was unbearable. Jesse's eyes started to water. They began to feel like two eggs boiling in their sockets. The synthetic fibers of his costume had wilted and now threatened to bond with his flesh. The smoke grew thick. Jesse coughed, feeling the weight of Tanya's body barrel into his as she gave him a hard shove toward the rear exit.

Outside the restaurant, he remained transfixed by the fire, like a bug inside a lamp shade. His heart fluttered like the wings of a disoriented Gypsy Moth until Tanya's foot connected with his rear end, which sent him stumbling across the parking lot. He regained his balance, then followed her across the field from where they'd come.

The restaurant was already engulfed by the time they got halfway across the field. He stopped to marvel at the magma

projectiles, lapping at the night sky as they coiled around the roof-
top.

"Move it!" Tanya thumped him across his furry back.

***

The five-alarm blaze caught Gerald off guard when he pulled
into Big Bang Burrito's parking lot. He nearly side-swiped the dumpster while forgetting to hit the emergency break. The work van
rolled back slightly as he tumbled out of the driver's side and then
booked it across the lot.

As predicted, the tool belt sat on a boulder, under the saguaro—
a three pronged giant, a totem, a needle god silhouetted against
the fuming inferno. Gerald snatched the tool bag and was about to
return to the van, to dial the police, when he found himself unable
to move—despite the incredible heat. His knees had morphed into
two blobs of putty. His legs had refused to support the upper half of
his beefy countenance—and so he collapsed onto the boulder, under the saguaro, his jaw unhinged in dumfounded disbelief, his face
feeling like a campfire marshmallow, ready to slide off its stick.

*One of the jackety-ass electricians did his job incorrectly and I'm
sure as hell not taking the rap for it!* He was willing to bet that Mitch
was to blame for the misstep.

Cruisers and firetrucks had roared into the lot but Gerald hardly
noticed. His eyes had begun to burn and to water as he—now no
longer sure whether to laugh or to cry or to shrug—marveled over
the idea that a project, which took his crew many weeks to build—a
project worth hundreds of thousands of dollars in building material—could be snuffed out in a matter of minutes.

The area surrounding Big Bang Burrito grew blacker than black,
as if the five-alarm blaze had consumed itself and was now becoming a dying star. The blackness was then
followed by a searing white flash. The parking lot, and the field
surrounding it, flickered in a ghastly silver glow followed by a sonic
boom. The fryolator produced an ungodly BANG, similar to the
sound of a quarter stick going off—maybe even louder, like the
sound of a launching space shuttle.

Black and purple plumes soared in one sweeping column, due
to the force, caused by an updraft, which had sucked, pulled and
gathered sand, dust and other debris within a 20-yard circumfer-

ence, and then shot it into the air in one massive projectile. The result: a brown and gray cloud resembling a head of cauliflower.

On the other edge of the field, Tanya was nearly wetting her pants from a feeling of exaltation. The high was to her what the first time mainlining was like for a smack user— and even though Jesse was quite a ways from the scene, he could still feel the ground quake. He nearly tripped over his own feet trying to keep up with Tanya, who had already reached the crest of the ravine.

Back at the restaurant, a deafening explosion filled Gerald's ears. The wind velocity had by this time packed so much punch, it caused the saguaro to bend at a 30-degree angle before toppling onto Gerald. His final breath, before he was flattened under the weight of the prickly beast, was having to reckon with one very pissed off cactus, coming at him with its outstretched arms. Witnesses at the scene would later swear that they'd heard the cactus growl before it descended upon Gerald.

Another BOOM followed, shaking the ground. Fire trucks and cop cruisers rocked from the force. Big Bang Burrito's roof fell away in thick ashy bits. Chunks of concrete pelted the Timorlan work van, dinging the roof and cracking the windshield. A piece of the roof came barreling down from the sky, flattening the van's front bumper.

Booms roared in the ears of the police officers and the firemen—flames lapped at their nomex suits as watery geysers shot from the ends of their hoses to snuff out the fire that'd turned a toxic blue-green from the building's charred materials. The air reeked of creosote and of other undefinable chemical smells.

The folks that were living across the street had set up chairs on the stoops of their newly constructed McMansions to ogle the scene in their pajamas. The explosions had reverberated like an amplified bass drum in their chests. They texted their neighbors, who, sitting just several feet away on the adjacent stoop, texted them back. They made lots of comments in regards to the rumpus in front of them, accompanied with the following emoticons:

:-\   □- (:-o   :-?   >:-l   >:-(

    Some folks snapped photos with their smartphones, later to be posted on Instagram. Others shot videos, to be posted on Youtube. These, along with a slew of selfies—fire and smoke used as a backdrop—would later be posted to Facebook walls. Each would be accompanied with sentiments such as OMG and WTF, along with a string of emojis.

    One of the oglers, a 17-year-old who'd just been hired for a cashier position at the new Big Bang Burrito, sat on his stoop posting a Facebook message to his wall:

Scott Free: Dudes, Im wachin my workpacle cross the street brun down 2 the grond...looks like sumthing frum Hunger Game's Caching Fire, man!!!   :-o

8 Seconds ago
Like - Comment - Share
30 people like this.

Justin Case: That sux.
7 Seconds ago - Like

Dan Drift: Man, th must suc, dude.
6 Seconds ago - Like

Pete Moss Wow, itnense, Scotty...my thuts goout to you, bro.
5 Seconds: ago - Like

Scott Free: Yep...& I wuz 2 strt wrking thecounter thiss Fri....seems 2 B the kinda year I been having. >.<

Justin Case: :(
4 Seconds ago - like

Dan Drift: :(:(
3 Seconds ago - like

Pete Moss: :(:(:(
2 Seconds ago - like

73

Scott Free: Thanx all, 4 yore s'port...Piece out!
1 Second ago - like
Write a comment...

***

From the opposite edge of the field, Tanya listened to the explosions as she wiggled out of her ape costume, and then stuffed it into the crack of the nearest boulder. The sound was like music to her ears. *This one's for you, Daddy.* With her mind elsewhere, she forgot about Jesse and scrambled into the dry creek bed.

WHOOP! WHOOP!

A boom, followed by a rumble, awakened Faith, who'd dozed off into a sugar coma. A soft glow, radiating from somewhere on the horizon, illuminated her studio apartment and rousted her from her bed. She knocked the Magic 8 Ball off of the stand. It rolled across the hardwood floor, stopping at her feet as she looked out the window. Rust-red plumes rose in the distance. A fire truck and three police cruisers screamed past.

They did it...and I did nothing to help them. Wondering how Tanya and Jesse were faring, Faith looked glumly down at her feet, where the Magic 8 ball lay.

Outlook Not So Good.

Back in the field, Jesse felt his knees tremble. His heart crashed in his chest as he paused to catch his breath at the edge of the ravine. Tanya was already in the car. He could tell from the glow of the taillights that she had started the engine. He would join her in a minute, he just needed some air. His thin chest hitched ever-so-slightly as he took gulps of the chilled night air.

Two cars were barreling up Turkey Buzzard Road and were headed toward the pullout as Jesse was about to descend into the ravine. They looked as if they had ski racks on their roofs, but when they drew closer and began to slow down, he could tell, by the light of the moon, that they were cop cruisers. They slowed to a crawl as they reached the pull out. This was when his bladder let go.

Back at the car, Tanya began to wonder where in hell Jesse was. He'd been right behind her...or so she thought. Had he bailed on her?

She drummed her fingers on the steering wheel and revved the engine. When she glanced in her rearview mirror, she noticed several dots of silver light bobbing in the dark. They grew from being the size of number two pencil erasers, to the size of golf balls—and then grew bigger, then bigger still. It took a moment for her mind to register that the orbs were actually people with flashlights and that they were inching toward her rear bumper.

From the red glow of the taillights, she could make out a group of men dressed in police uniform. She stomped the gas. She tried to hightail it down the creek bed, but didn't get far when her tires hit a silty patch and began to spin in place. The tires sank several inches, kicking up sand and dust. The smell of burning rubber filled the interior of the sedan.

From the top of the ravine, Jesse observed the officers approaching the sedan. He bolted back into the field, heading southeast by foot, away from the ravine. The polyester lining of his ape regalia made him itchy. Its voluminosity impeded his step. Heavy to begin with, it'd become downright cumbersome with the added weight of sweat and urine.

He would have stripped out of the damned thing, except that he wasn't wearing anything underneath, just tube socks and a pair of boxers. Thinking that he'd be too hot wearing both his clothes and the ape suit, he'd opted to leave his change of clothes in the car.

He moaned while clutching his side. Tonight hadn't turned out as glamorous as he'd anticipated. Sure, the fryolator going up in flames had made for a great explosion—better than any he'd seen in an Arnold Schwarzenegger flick—or the one he'd pictured while reading the Edward Abbey novel, but what happened back there was not only not fiction, it was totally fucking illegal—and it was absolutely, hands down, the stupidest thing he'd ever gotten involved with.

He would distance himself from Tanya, starting now. No one would need know that he was involved with this fire. He hadn't even been the one to pour the gasoline or to light the match. Hopefully Faith hadn't—and wouldn't—go around blabbing to others about their little plot. *Hopefully...Man, Tanya's gonna roast for this one.* What if she squealed on him?

Back at the car, Tanya tasted the burning rubber on her tongue and understood then that it was useless to even try, that the sedan would not budge. Nevertheless her foot remained on the gas: VVVVRRROOOMMM.

"Damn it!" Tanya pounded the steering wheel. She'd be busted for the stolen car—that wouldn't be such a big deal—an easy bailout from Daddy—but if she were to be linked with those fires...? And Jesse...? *The wimpy little weasel probably took off...he better not breathe a word about our stunt or I'm gonna have to commit murder, too...it doesn't matter...I can get out of this. I can get out of anything.*

She was glad she'd ditched the ape costume, along with the gasoline jugs, which she'd ditched in Big Bang Burrito's kitchen. However, she wished that she'd heeded Jesse's warning about not parking in the washout—especially since she knew, from personal experience, that one cannot drive anywhere on the planet one desires, just because one has all-wheel drive.

Case in point, for their first—and last—father and daughter outing, Tanya and Ron had stayed at a ClubMed in Sandpiper Bay. There, they swam and played lots of tennis, but then Ron wanted to try his hand at fly-fishing. He'd talked Tanya into going on an excursion through the Florida swamps—he had either been watching too many action movies, too many car commercials, or was simply experiencing a midlife meltdown, because if he'd had any sense, he'd have known that one can't exactly trailblaze through a mangrove forest.

Tanya and Ron had ended up on the edge of a swamp after Ron decided to take a short cut by pulling off the road designated for park visitors, and onto a road which had signs posted everywhere that said:

WILDLIFE SANCTUARY
NO MOTOR VEHICLES

Tanya had started to gag on the flatulent bog stench, which rose thick in the Florida heat. From there, things had gone downhill pretty quickly. Tanya and Ron had had to climb out of their windows while the truck slowly sank into the earth. The angry mud gods had devoured the tires, then the flatbed, and finally the front bumper. Air bubbles had gurgled their gushy gurgling sounds as Ron Kendrick's powerful mean machine was suctioned into the viscous brown sludge which stank of frog eggs and sulfur.

Tanya and her father found themselves stranded on the roof of the truck. They clutched the mossy cypress bows that'd dripped above, in order to balance themselves as they struggled not to slide off the roof and down the windshield, which was slicked with mud. Ron was on his smartphone and was screaming at AAA while Tanya fended off the alligators by dropping F bombs and swinging her tennis racket. The tennis racket had connected with one very persistent alligator that'd snapped at her pant leg, missed, and came away with the truck's antenna instead.

Tanya and Ron were promptly rescued by two bearded men in overalls, who happened to be buzzing down the waterway in their motor-powered rowboat. The men scared the alligators away with their shotguns. A tow truck had later hauled Ron's brand-new Ford F-350 out of the bog.

***

What on God's blue planet is taking them so long? Surely Tanya couldn't have gone that far, thought Ginger sitting in her La-Z-Boy with Freddy in her lap, sipping a glass of prune juice and waiting to hear back from the Yucca Police Department. Ginger noticed a noxious burning smell and wondered if it was coming from inside the house.

Freddy smelled it too. He leapt to the floor. He paced, then meowed once before leaping onto the windowsill. He poked his head between the curtains. Outside, in the distance, there was a fire bigger than any he'd ever seen, and lights—lots of lights, scintillating atop of big hunks of metal, the kind of lights Freddy associated with trouble.

For a change it was trouble he need not concern himself with. In fact, he had a feeling that from here on out the major hassle in his life: the Girl, along with her awful smell and noisy footsteps, would soon be gone. He would celebrate by rolling in a pile of high-grade catnip.

***

Back at the ravine, four officers were closing in on the sedan: two on one side, two on the other. Their faces, glowing in the beams of their mag lights, contrasted sharply with the dark night. To Tanya, their faces resembled zombie masks. One of the masks floated in the driver's side window. A pale fist wrapped on the glass—a gesture for Tanya to roll down her window. She obliged and, smiling at the zombie mask, asked, "Is something the matter?"

Back in the field, the moon was descending in the west as Jesse approached the bottom of Turkey Buzzard Road, where it looped into the downtown section. The sky, a deep shade of cobalt, had faded to a rich shade of periwinkle, signaling dawn's approach. The neon signs seemed not to notice. They continued to blaze as if the night would go on forever. Jesse's eyes were overwhelmed by the neon forrest of advertisements:

24HR DINER
CAR WASH
MOTEL: NO VACANCY
XXX
GIRLS GIRLS GIRLS
SEX, SEX, SEX
DRIVE THROUGH
CABLE TV
WI FI
BEER PONG
BOWLING
TIKI BAR
TATTOO
EAT PIE
YUCCA CHEVROLET.

1-800-WARP

Another fire truck roared past Faith's apartment. She thought she could hear a helicopter purring above. *Oh goodie, maybe I won't have to work tomorrow! Maybe, thinking that our restaurant will be the next to go, my boss'll be too terrified to stay in operation and will give everyone the day off!*

She discovered, however, that she needn't worry about work. When she checked her Facebook newsfeed, she discovered that she'd been fired. One of her co-workers had posted: good 2 C that slacker gon!! :). The post had received 20 Likes in response. Faith wasn't surprised. She would later call Mom for some money.

A police cruiser breezed by. Its siren was on silent but its lights had cast stuttering blue patterns on Faith's walls. Daylight had bleached the periwinkle sky to a lighter blue. In the western part of the sky, a swirling column of smoke stretched like taffy into the upper stratosphere before spreading like cheese cloth over downtown Yucca.

Thinking about how much work it must have taken Tanya and Jesse to pull the job, Faith yawned and returned to bed, content in the idea that she'd saved herself a whole lot of hassle. She flipped through the TV channels. The usual informercials were on: the Cellulite Snatcher on channel 001.

Faith had canceled her gym membership when Todd got her the Cellulite Snatcher for her birthday. The device came in two colors, beige or baby blue. At first she thought Todd had gotten her a vibrator, but when she removed the gift from its packaging, she saw that it looked more like a landline telephone receiver with a chord that plugged into the wall.

There were two dials located on what looked like the speaking end of the receiver-like device. The first dial was labeled VIBRATION SPEED. Its choice of settings were as follows:

SLOW   MEDIUM   FAST   JACKHAMMER

SANDBLAST   TURBOJET

The second dial was labeled SUCTION STRENGTH. Its choice of settings were as follows:

GENTLE   MEDIUM-GENTLE   NOT-SO-GENTLE

HOOVER-MANEUVER

GRAVITATIONAL PULL   EVENT HORIZON

There was a miniature-sized motor mounted inside of what looked like the listening end of the receiver-like device, with grooves for screwing on the attachment heads. The Cellulite Snatcher came with two heads: one with bristles stiffer than those on a windshield scraper—the other with tiny suction cups that vaguely resembled the underside of a squid.

The vibration speed corresponded with the brush attachment, which controlled the device's scouring strength. The suction dial controlled the strength of the cups' suctioning ability. An instruction manual, in 20 different languages, showed two-dimensional illustrations of women's bellies, buttocks and hips, with tiny black dots denoting the cellulite clusters. The manual then gave the recommended settings for said problem areas.

"The vibration and the brush bristles stimulate the epidermis, which in turn, wakens the dermis, which in turn, gets those fat cells moving...think of rocks bouncing around inside of a rock tumbler, ladies!! Over time they grow smooth... over time those stubborn adipocytes shrink to the size of ice cream jimmies," the television actress with a spray tan and bleached teeth blathered at Faith. "The suction stimulates those fat lobes, which are that gelatinous mass that holds all those little jimmies together...for that hard-to-remove cellulite, I recommend adjusting your dial to Event Horizon...I am telling you ladies this-product-has-changed-my-life...and it'll change yours, too!!"

The product was a monumental failure and the cause of Faith's worst fight with Todd. The Hoover Maneuver setting had been useless, yet the Gravitational Pull—never mind Event Horizon—actually hurt. She thought for sure her skin would be sucked right off her bones. By the end of the week, she was left with a row of hickeys on her left buttock. Todd had then accused her of cheating on him.

Faith flipped the channel. She yawned. A telethon, asking for donations to support the Wounded Anteater Reservation Project, grabbed her attention. The telethon boasted camera shots of an anteater sanctuary, located on a grassy savanna in a country whose name Faith couldn't pronounce. The television camera panned on several creatures, corralled inside a cage made from chicken wire, with faces resembling vacuum nozzles and hind ends like feather dusters. With eyes beadier than sweater buttons, they gazed entreatingly at their television audience.

Unlike the bubble brained actress in the Cellulite Snatcher informercial, the actress for the WARP telethon bore a rather grave expression, her complexion appearing as if it hadn't seen a single ray of Vitamin D for over a decade. "These furry four-legged friends need your support," she implored as the news ticker left a hotline number for those wishing to volunteer:

1-800-WARP
www.woundedanteater.org

The anteaters' beady little eyes melted Faith's heart. She rolled out of bed to retrieve her cell phone.

***

Jesse thought that by now he and Tanya would be having a toast, would be clinking their frosty malt tumblers together: "To us!" He thought they'd be relishing the brain-paralyzing effects of an ice cream headache as they chugged down sweet, icy beverages—before calling it a night, where Jesse would then snuggle in for a deep and restful sleep among his down pillows, dotted with sheep serenading him with their fiddles for the good deed he'd done.

Instead, he was alone and coated with sweat and desert dust. The furry legs of his ape suit were full of cholla needles. What's worse, he thought he heard a police chopper. Its staccato-like thrum grew louder as it orbited the field. Jesse tried to outrun it but only got as far as the edge of the field where Turkey Buzzard Road and Route 15 met.

The giant, steel dragonfly now hovered directly above, ready to descend on Jesse as he found himself bathed in the blue beam of its searchlight. The mesquite grass rippled wildly in the breeze, reminding Jesse of the stills in that photo book of Yucca during the

1960s. The chopper hovered a moment longer before re-treating into the sky.

Jesse thought he was home free, although his heart banged wildly in his ribs and his knees threatened to buckle as he mustered the strength to dart into Route 15's cross-walk. There, he was intercepted by a cop cruiser—its paint job black as Darth Vader—flashing its red, white and blues:

WHOOP! WHOOP!

The cruiser kicked up a menacing breeze as it revved its engine, and then squealed its tires as it eclipsed Jesse in the crosswalk. "Freeeeeezzze! Put. Your. Paws. Where. I. Can. See. Them!!" An officer dragooned over the bullhorn.

Nature Boy

After being booked, Tanya dialed her father, who picked up on the first ring.

"It's me, Dad."

".. ... .?"

"Yeah, I know it's 4:30 in the morning—"

".. ...."

"Yeah, I know, it's the tenth time this year—"

"... ....!"

"I don't know why I did it, I just did. It's not my fault the cops arrested me—"

"... ....?!"

"The cops are overreacting—"

".. ....?"

"I don't freaking know. Why don't you ask them!?"

"....... .. ..!! ... ...?"

"I don't know why I stole the car!"

Tanya wanted to tell her father that stealing things helped her to feel calm, but didn't dare. He might get mad and stop loving her.

"I didn't have a car and I needed to go somewhere—"

"...., ..., ..."

"I know I haven't bothered to visit Mom, but she and I hate each other...Really...?" (tone suddenly sweet) "You'll help me post bail?"

".. ..."

"You're the best!"

***

Jesse was thankful for his thick fur. Had it not been for that, he felt certain those handcuffs would have bitten into his wrists—he'd seen Gerald's wrists after he'd been arrested once, and it wasn't pretty.

"Suspicious ape, detaining suspect, expedite 10-48, over," said the officer in the driver's seat.

The strobing blue lights hurt Jesse's eyes. A sizzling, static-filled voice from the radio, filled the interior of the cruiser:

`~!@#$%^&*()-_=+<>/\...

"Say again?"
CRACKLE. SIZZLE:

`~!@#$%^&*()-_=+<>/\| !!

"I've got an ape in custody. Do you copy?"

CRACKLE. SIZZLE:

`~!@#$%^&*()-_=+<>/\|...`~!@#$%^&*()-_=+<>/\|.

"Affirmative. Out—"
"But I wasn't the one that did it!!" Jesse whined. "I only—
"I'd shut my cake hole if I were you, Chewbacca," said the officer in the driver's seat.
"Yeah, you furry primate. I hear where you're going, they serve lots of banana pudding for dessert," said the officer in the passenger's seat.
"But, but...you didn't even read me my...my..." Jesse struggled to remember that fancy word associated with the right to remain silent. "My...uh...veranda rights—"
The officers howled with laughter. Jesse didn't know why, yet understood that the joke was on him. His cheeks blazed. They'd already humiliated him enough when they groped his furry physique in search of a deadly weapon, drugs or anything else they could incriminate him with.
He wondered why they were nothing like they were in the TV show Cops, where the officers seemed patient, almost gallant as they dutifully protected the public from some meth head with pitted teeth—eyeballs boinging out of his sockets like the coils of a mattress, while having a freakout—or from some boozer babbling nonsense, his words running together like watercolor paints on a doodle pad while urinating in public—or from some wife who had allegedly beaned her husband over the head with a carpet sweeper, her diatribes disturbing the neighbors on the other side of her wall.
Of course this would all be filmed before a live television audience, of course the officers would attempt to reason with these not-so-wholesome, all-American lost causes, before calmly placing them in cuffs and guiding

them into the rear of the cruiser—while gracefully enduring nasty epithets—one of them referring to a certain animal species, that begins with the letter P, associated with America's favorite breakfast meat—but that the show's editor would later omit, using a big fat BEEEEEEEEEEEP.

There were no beeps to cover the locker room talk that'd escaped the lips of Hank and Mitch—Jesse learned the names of his arresting officers because they'd been mentioned over the cop radio—and no, they were nothing like the cops in Cops, because they wouldn't let up on him. First, they called him Chewbacca, then Donkey Kong, before finally settling on Koko.

"What the fuck smells, Koko? You smell like a veterinary clinic, boy!" said Mitch, the officer in the passenger's seat, who offered him one of their donuts: banana cream. Jesse had no appetite—he was surprised that he hadn't wet himself again.

"Better eat up, Koko. That could be the last donut you'll eat in the free world, or the last donut you'll eat for a long, long time. I don't think they serve donuts in prison." Mitch turned to look at Jesse for the first time as they looped westward, toward the Big Bang Burrito disaster.

Jesse noted how sharp and pointed Mitch's nose was. There was nothing soft about his profile, which looked as if it'd been whittled from a block of wood—there was nothing soft about Hank's either. Both of the men wore their hair buzzed. Hank's fat neck was dotted with pimples from having received a lousy razor job.

Why do they all wear a buzz? Jesse wondered as they slowed to a crawl. Hank stomped the break and they jerked forward. An emergency vehicle in front of them had stopped unexpectedly.

Big Bang Burrito's foundation had been reduced to a charbroiled stump. A few tatty two-by-fours were all that remained of the cookie-cutter establishment. Jesse wished he could smile, wished he could pat himself on the back—and maybe he would have, if he'd gotten away with the thing that he didn't technically do. Although maybe not. The two-by-fours—the ones that had maintained their vertical position—were nothing but a lopsided stand of blackened, twisted, skeletal fingers jutting toward the sky, as if beckoning for it to hold them up as they struggled not to cave in on themselves.

Jesse coughed. The air stank. The smoke contrails were tinted with rust-brown hues. Fine ash particles blew on the morning currents like bits of confetti. The toxic ash wouldn't remain just at the site, it would blow for miles. It'd blow all over Yucca and beyond, leaving a thin, gray gauze. The cremated remains of the corporate box would go on to coat the desert landscape like a fine powdered sugar.

The sugar would be barely visible to the eye, if visible at all, yet the cacti, the mesquite bushes and the lizards would be covered with the stuff—and the insects, too, which in turn would be eaten by the lizards.

Now all the lizards are gonna die!! Acid climbed up Jesse's esophagus.

The tragic consequences reminded Jesse of Silent Spring by Rachel Carson, who tried to warn the public about the dangers of parathion, about the dangers it posed to the birds who would eat the worms, which were coated in the stuff—like Gummi Worms rolled in sugar—and then die.

An ambulance pulled out in front of them. Did a fireman get hurt trying to put out the fire? Jesse became confused when he saw the Timorlan work van in the lot. *Why is that there? I thought Dad and Gerald had already finished the job....* He recognized the van because no one else in Yucca, that he knew of, had a van with the mudflap girl painted on its sliding door.

The van's entire front end was caved in: the windshield, the radiator grill, the headlights...the bumper was mashed into the blacktop, squashed like a Little Debbie cupcake.

***

The bars of the jail cell had cast shadows on Tanya's sullen face. She sat with her knees up on the concrete floor, her back to the pink wall, half-expecting to see a Barbie-themed, lace canopy in the corner of the holding cell.

Instead, there was a wood bench occupied by one very drunk woman wearing a Wonder Woman costume. The woman didn't annoy Tanya, neither did Wonder Woman, but the pink walls sure did. *Green is not for girls!* Tanya could picture Donna's flaring nostrils. And it made her want to vape but there was no vaping permitted inside any indoor structure, private or public. Yucca recently passed the law to include one's own home and vehicle. It was in the process of passing the law to include all outdoor spaces including, but not limited to: traffic medians, under trees, around shrubs, under street lamps, and anywhere within 3,000 feet of a smiling infant—or within 6,000 feet of a bawling infant. Vape pens were legal—Yucca's residents were allowed to possess up to one vape pen—they just weren't allowed to vape their vape pens.

***

Hank and Mitch had been disappointed when they'd found zilch on Jesse, after having frisked him before loading him into the cruiser—although dumbfounded by what they saw when they yanked off his rubber mask—the big bad arsonist that'd been terrorizing Cholla County for months was, in reality, a meek, doleful, doe-faced boy.

Determined to find something that they could incriminate the little goober with, they'd ordered Jesse to strip down at the county jail, but were instantly put off by his semi-naked body, which was as pasty and thin as a cooked spaghetti noodle—and hairless except for the scrappy patch of copper-colored hair that'd appeared as if it'd been glued to his chest.

They then insisted that he remove his foot gear, and were even more disappointed when all they discovered was a worry stone that'd rolled to the toe of one tube sock, and a Tofutti Cutie wrapper stuffed in the band of the other tube sock—the one with a hole in its toe which had exposed Jesse's ingrown toenail. "I don't believe in littering," he'd told Hank when Hank had inquired about the dairy-free dessert wrapper.

"I don't believe in littering," Hank would later mock Jesse to the other officers during their 6 a.m. coffee break. "We picked up a real doozy. Turns out our arsonist's not only a suburbanite dweeb, but a bonafide nature boy. I honestly can't say I've encountered a criminal quite like `im...and that ape suit...? That thing stank to high hell. The apes I've seen at the zoo actually smell better than that kid did! And I really didn't need to see those wet boxers—I told him to get back in the ape suit and to make it snappy."

***

It was nearly 5:30 a.m. when Jesse was granted his one phone call.

"D...uh...D Dad??"

".....?!!"

"Uh...um...yeah, uh...it's me...uh—"

"..... ... ...? ....! ....!!"

"Gerald's...um...dead?"

"...!"

"Uh...oh...oh...why...um...how?"

A superfluous question, since the memory of the work van's mangled front end came rushing at Jesse the second the word "dead" crackled from the other end of the line. By asking that question in that stammering stuttering tongue of his, he felt like the stupidest Homo sapien to walk the planet.

"A...piece of the...roof squashed the...top of the work van...but the paramedics believe Gerald was...attacked by the saguaro...cops think the force from the explosion caused the thing to fall on `im..." Jesse could hear Dad splutter between sniffling, hiccuping sobs.

Last night's sentiment, I wish he was dead, was like a sliver of glass that jabbed Jesse's conscience. "I wish I was dead," Jesse mumbled, hanging up the phone.

Too Many Apes

Ginger read The Yucca Bugler over coffee while Freddy purred at her feet. The two were waiting for Ginger's sedan to be returned to her in one piece. She'd already met with two officers, one of whom she'd communicated with in sign language—they'd showed up at 8 a.m. and had asked her endless questions regarding the stolen vehicle, the ape sightings and her allegation that Tanya had been the culprit behind all the fires.

***

Tanya was, indeed, the car thief. That much the YPD had confirmed. Tanya was now awaiting arraignment, and would likely be charged with grand larceny. This afternoon, the YPD planned to debrief Tanya on grounds of suspected arson.

Meanwhile, they wished to hear Ginger's recount of all the events that had taken place in the night—the ape getting away in the sedan and so forth—but they wished to hear more about the items Ginger found in Tanya's room, and about what she knew of Tanya's character.

The YPD was beginning to suspect that they either had the wrong ape in custody—since many trick or treaters decided to go as an ape for Halloween—or that there had been more than one ape involved in the arsons. Nevertheless, they needed to be thorough, especially since the 911 call Ginger had made on her operator relay service was barely comprehendible.

The dispatcher thought that Ginger Hale seemed quite hysterical. Anyone reading her message, which she must have typed with two very shaky hands, could sense her panic, which came out in a myriad of typos: misspellings, poor grammar, improper punctuation, forgetting to capitalize, run-on sentences, dangling modifiers—the message lacked smooth transitions from one idea to the next. In fact, the operator came away feeling that Ginger's emergency call lacked a clear premise. Obviously the woman had never been exposed to the Common Core Standards in English Language Arts:

Help1 HELP@ yELP! No sure it's brake'n rot...
but saw ape black furry think at me frum bed4oom door

it size of man aynd slipt out door. it slain Freddy's face
out aynd Got away in me Sedan.
2 nite I goes to base ment aynd checks in on T.
futon aynd blankets. they pulled back, but
no indent of T. no sleep, but no Tan6a, they
just knead make shur that ape black and furry
think no Tanya have stollen me Sedan.

help! yelp1! I rezide with nut! T isthe
firebug of Cholla County!

Though the interview with Ginger led the YPD to wonder
if Tanya Kendrick was one of the arsonists involved, if not
the arsonist, they still needed to conduct further investiga-
tion—especially since Ginger's assertion that Tanya had
shapeshifted into an ape, while at the same admitting she'd
popped too many Lunesta tablets at bedtime—didn't instill
much confidence in them.

They'd considered the fact that four of their officers had
traced Ginger's sedan to a washed-out creek, not far from
the fire. Tanya having tried to outrun them made her look
mighty guilty. Still, she was found wearing only her street
clothes. The police hadn't found an ape suit in the car or
anywhere near it, nor did they find one at the scene of the
crime. When questioned about the gym bag of clothes on
the passenger seat, Tanya had replied blithely, "My boy-
friend's clothes. He'd left them at my house."

***

The headline and photos on the cover of The Yucca
Bugler startled Ginger:

Twenty Nine-Year-Old Man Killed By Falling
Saguaro: Arsonist May Face
Involuntary Manslaughter.

Yucca, A.Z. twenty-year-old suspect, caught wearing
Big Foot gear, was arrested for setting fire to Big Bang Burrito. He is now in Cholla County Jail awaiting arraignment. "I

didn't do it," he said, and broke down in tears when asked if he felt any remorse for the death of his brother.

Ginger had been eating toast. She stopped chewing when she saw the mugshot. *Jimminy shit Crickets! It's the boy that was here the other day. We'd shaken hands.* Nothing about his touch, which was so gentle, could ever convince her that he was capable of such an act.

There was an aerial photo on page A2 of a Big Foot-like creature running toward the edge of a field. Ginger shook her head. She flipped to the next page. Toward the back of the newspaper, there existed just a tiny blurb about Tanya and the stolen vehicle.

Ginger's mind was starting to reel. Too many apes, too many crimes—and not enough police. Sighing, she tossed the paper down.

She'd been convinced that the ape was Tanya, but now she was not so sure. One thing she was sure of was this, she no longer felt safe in Yucca, which had been the case for a while, but now she felt even less so.

Freddy continued to doze at her feet. Through the thin material of her terrycloth slippers, she could feel him purr. She envied him.

I Am Ape, Hear Me Roar

The Yucca Police Department never could confirm whether or not there had been more than one ape involved in the burning of Big Bang Burrito. Tanya and Jesse slogged through two years of court trials before they were finally acquitted of second-degree arson, involuntary manslaughter and trespassing, due to insufficient evidence. No one, besides Ginger Hale, had furnished the police department with further information.

Though free to roam the streets of Yucca, Tanya and Jesse were held in captivity in the sense that the YPD, from that day forward, would be watching them. Meanwhile, the lack of fires in the town of Yucca since that fateful Halloween had given its residents peace of mind.

Though Yucca had managed to fall into a state of tranquility, the same could not be said for other cities across the southeastern United States, where ape pockets had begun to multiply by the dozen, followed by five-alarm blazes that continued to crop up like volcanic arcs in the Pacific Ocean.

***

Faith Waverly spent the greater part of the day laying around in a sugar daze in front of the tube. Her 31st birthday had passed and she'd eaten too much cake. Not much was on TV, the Cellulite Snatcher infomercial, along with the anteater telethon, had long since stopped airing—although she'd saved the 1-800 number for the Wounded Anteater Reservation Project. It was pinned to her cork board over her long list of New Year's resolutions.

She rolled out of bed, tempted to call the 1-800 number. She'd dialed it two years ago, hours after Big Bang Burrito had burned down. She'd been gung-ho about volunteering until the executive director told her that the position would entail—besides relocating to South America—spoon feeding dog kibble laced with ants, grubs and termites to the anteaters and mucking their pens, and giving them distemper shots. Faith's idea of volunteering for WARP would have involved posting pictures of anteaters to her Facebook wall, or getting her Facebook friends to "Like" WARP's page. She hung up when the executive director recommended she get a rabies vaccination before leaving the U.S.

She had to shake the Magic 8 Ball before deciding whether or not to call. It would mark her tenth shake in one day. The first five concerned whether or not she should carry her fetid, reeking garbage out to the dumpster today, or let it go for another week. The next four shakes concerned whether or not she should shower or brush her teeth first.

Faith grabbed the toy off her stand. She paused. Before she could ask it whether or not she should dial the 1-800 number, she needed to know just one more thing:

Will I ever find direction in life?

For this question, she gave the ball a hearty shake.

I wish this chick would donate me to the Salvation Army so some little kid can take me home. I bet the little kid would better understand the concept of what I am and what I can do, versus what I am not and what I cannot do. I cannot even get three hour's rest without being shook so hard I feel as if I am about to have a hemorrhage—forget the Salvation Army, just toss me into the garbage, please!

As Faith waited eagerly, the ball released its die where it floated toward the watery window to deliver her its prophecy. The die had been moving more sluggishly these days. The ball's liquid innards, once a lovely shade of Toilet Duck blue, had faded to a dishwater gray, dotted with fizzy air pockets that made the message difficult for Faith to read.

Don't count on it.

So insulted was Faith, she tossed the Magic 8 Ball into her fetid, reeking wastebasket and then hauled the entire thing out of her kitchen.

Why not South America? Faith asked herself, fuming as she bumped her way down the stairwell and across the tenant parking lot. At the dumpster, she paused. She stared into the wastebasket. The ball, nestled in a mound of wadded up tissue, chicken bones and pizza crusts, beamed up at her.

She tied the bag and tossed it, Magic 8 Ball and all, into the dumpster. Why not South America?

102

"Why not the southeastern United States?" the voice of news anchor Alison Au'Gratin continued to drift from Faith's television while she took out the trash. "It's hard to know if these ape arsonist impersonators are inspired by the actions of Tanya Kendrick and Jesse Timorlan—the two youths of Yucca, who were tried and later acquitted for second-degree arson and involuntary manslaughter in the Big Bang Burrito case, or if they were simply influenced by the ever increasing violence of video games.

"Sprawl communities, seem to be hit the hardest with incidents of arson. Some residents fear that arsonist ape colonies are now part of a nationwide cult which seems to be making its way toward the eastern states—wiping out would-be chain restaurants in its wake.

"Big Bang Burrito and similar businesses seem to be the prime target. Dominick's Donuts, of Noland, Maryland, tries to remain positive despite that its five would-be stores have been destroyed by five-alarm blazes. With 40 other stores currently in operation, the business remains optimistic about a possible financial rebound for the fiscal year of 2017. It is currently reaping benefits from the Big Box Emergency Relief Fund.

"Still, the folks of Noland, Maryland, are on edge, especially since the police continue to discover eerie messages, spray painted on the blacktop of every Dominick's Donuts' parking lot:

I am ape, hear me roar.

"Meanwhile, Big Bang Burrito is still going strong. Cholla County, where it'd built its flagship restaurant back in 1990, now boasts 70 restaurants total—Yucca alone, now has seven.

"Still, should the cults and burnings continue, Governor Guillermo Gonad has promised to send in the National Guard. For anyone watching this, my advice is this: If you see something, say something."

Faith returned from the dumpster in time to catch the end of the news blurb. Tired of hearing about Tanya and Jesse and the fires, she rolled her eyes. *I can't hear myself think.* She hit POWER on the TV and the screen went black. The air around her fell silent as she picked up the phone and dialed.

The End.

Winner of the Michael Doherty Award in Poetry, Amy Laprade's work has appeared in *Meat for Tea*: the *Valley Review*, *Canyon Voices, Plum Literary Journal* and *Write Angles Journal,* among others. Her debut novel, "So Nice to Finally Meet You..." was published by *Human Error Publishing*. "Behind the Magic 8 Ball" is her second novel.

To learn more about the author, go to www.amylaprade.com

So Nice to Finally Meet You...

By

Amy Laprade

Other books by Amy Laprade:

So Nice to Finally Meet You...

Estranged from her parents, fifteen-year-old Gina Laramee longs to understand her family roots and to have a normal, loving relationship with her mentally unstable Aunt Elaine, since Elaine is the closest thing to a mother Gina has—and is in fact closer than Gina realizes.
Published by Human Error Press, 2016.

Forthcoming in Spring 2019
Human Error Publishing

Silence Is Premeditated: a Collection

Silence

is a series of dots
that never converge
an elliptical cadence
of a conversation dropped due to a bad connection.
Speech impediments run in families. We stutter our
apologies.
Always, we say, I'm sorry
but never really mean it.
Silence is the understudy for such platitudes...

"Amy Laprade writes about contemporary life with a keen eye for gritty details in a way that nails the way we live in the 21st century. Readers can't help but be captivated by this romp of a read that veers from madcap to maddening mayhem."

~Hazel Dawkins,
Author of *Eyes on the Past*

"Behind The Magic 8 Ball is a comedy with serious undertones about two young social outcasts, Jesse and Faith, who get sucked into a quixotic plot to commit a crime for all the best reasons in a small Arizona town. One is reminded of early Jerry Lewis movies and Napoleon Dynamite."

~Richard Wayne Horton,
Two-time Pushcart nominee and author of *Artists In The Underworld* and *Sticks & Bones.*

"Amy Laprade weaves unforgettable characters into a story that carves hairpin turns in our perception. She shares an imagination that is at once unpredictable and yet deeply logical."

~Kathy Dunn,
Director - *Main Street Writers*

www.ingramcontent.com/pod-product-compliance
Lightning Source LLC
Chambersburg PA
CBHW071136250626
47159CB00006B/2243